CELESTIAL PHASE

THE FIFTH LUNAR LOVESCAPE NOVEL

ESSIE POWERS

PREPARATION ALGORITHM

*A*s always, prim and neat, dressed in her royal-blue overalls, Supervisor Mackenzie Angliss crossed her arms over her chest and sighed. She stood in her office, situated on one of the upper floors of the Lunar Grand Hotel. The walls of the office itself were glass, offering a view not only of the rest of the floor, but also of the Celestial Stays Dome landscape which surrounded her.

To begin with, she couldn't help but take in her image as projected in the glass.

Perhaps it was the dull quality of the reflection, but Mackenzie couldn't help thinking that her complexion looked washed out.

Pallid.

Her previously flame-red hair—what she'd always cherished as one of her *better* features—looked more akin to spoiled straw.

Even as she stood in front of the window, she couldn't help noticing that she was slouching slightly . . . that her figure was *bent*. At least that was something she could rectify right away.

She straightened up.

Once she'd got over her dowdy appearance, she found herself staring through the glass, in the direction of the Basements. The squat, half-buried building near the periphery of the Dome within which Celestial Stays employees were domiciled. Her own apartment was located there, too, of course. For want of a better term her 'home'.

As she drew her focus closer into the foreground, she took stock of the Crescent Gardens: a verdant ribbon snaking through the entirety of the Dome: Njhay Garcia's pride and joy, and the place which would play host to his and Louise William's wedding taking place in a few weeks' time. She could still recall the proposal—how she had had a hand in creating the scavenger hunt which'd eventually led to the engagement ring awaiting Louise.

She had said yes . . . obviously.

That reminded her.

Another thing which she had to organise.

Just to think of all the problems she had to solve sent her brain whirring.

She shifted her attention closer to the Lunar Grand.

The newly opened Stellar Tide Cultural Centre—run by Guardian Julius Denisov—caught her eye. Whereas before, it had housed a casino, the owner of Celestial Stays—Frau Karolin Köhler—had decided to shift the Dome away from commercial considerations, and to place a greater emphasis on other values. That was to say, at least how Mackenzie saw it, *community* values. Just what community Frau Köhler had in mind up here, on the Moon, Mackenzie really wouldn't like to so much as venture a guess.

Mackenzie skirted the periphery of the Dome now, taking in Entry Clearance, where the Lunar Shuttles and the Lunar Rovers were based. All those people coming and going—either headed back to Earth, or else off on some adventure across the lunar plains.

A little further along, there was the Orbital Café, with its prized view out over the lunar plains; perfect for taking in with a cup of coffee and a sugary snack . . . at least for those who *indulged* themselves in such things. Mackenzie had never been quite able to see the attraction herself. She had always prized her figure above all else.

And *certainly* above immediate gratification.

If she had decided, all those years ago, at the beginning of her career, that she wouldn't wait for anything—that she wouldn't have patience—then she never would've got anywhere.

Discipline was what her life was all about—*discipline* was the sole attribute which was responsible for her success.

Finally there was the Armstrong Archive, with its S-shaped building.

It was one of those buildings which—as Mackenzie knew only too well—housed a large amount of Earthside materials; a sort of extreme off-site backup solution. If anything happened down on Earth which might put paid to the entirety of the Link—and all remaining *physical* records—then there would at least be a good selection of resources with which to rebuild human knowledge.

If any humans remained, of course.

As she looked out over the sight—what she often thought of as *her* domain—her brain was nearly erupting. All those inner-workings. She could imagine every single moving part before her.

What most people didn't understand about her was just how *overwhelmed* she got—how there were nights when she found it impossible to sleep.

There were times when she *wished* she might somehow be

transported back home. Not to her *actual* home in Hammondville, New South Wales, Australia, but to the place where she had spent seemingly endless childhood holidays with her parents.

Her parents had had a beachfront home which looked out on the Indian Ocean; a home which was based in Western Australia— just outside Perth. It had been the perfect spot, sitting right on the sandy shore. The house itself had been filled with books and films. There were days when Mackenzie would simply spread her towel out on the front lawn, hunch her knees into her chest, and stare off across the flawless, sparkling sea.

Her parents, both successful, self-made business people, had placed great value in 'taking time away'. And since the two of them had always run their own businesses, booking time off was never a problem. Mackenzie supposed that she unconsciously utilised their time-efficiency techniques near enough every day.

Her *parents'* way of doing things was the main reason why she believed she'd been able to make a success of herself.

Back on Earth, she had built a consultancy firm—*graphic design*, of all things. She had managed to get hold of contracts with governments and large, multinational organisations. And all that despite being unable to so much as draw a decent smiley face herself. It had taken her only a little over two years before she'd been in a position to sell the business on, and to search for her next challenge. What had turned out to be Celestial Stays.

It was just as her parents had always liked to say.

All businesses were—in essence—the same.

In fact, 'business' was an abstract concept which really meant 'people'.

As long as you knew how to manage or—more cynically —*manipulate* people, then you could get along in just about any line of business you might imagine.

The key, at least as Mackenzie had identified it, was to know how to all at once keep people at an arm's length while breeding a sense of trust and confidence in yourself.

That, truly, was the recipe for success.

Even as Mackenzie stared out through the window, across the Celestial Stays Dome, she could feel the tears beginning to swill in her throat. She swallowed them back before it was too late.

Whenever she got to thinking about her parents, she couldn't help but recall the day they had died; when she had been *told* that they had died.

It had been one of those rarest of eventualities. Her parents had decided to attend an event together. Since they each had their own business—and in disparate areas—it wasn't often that they would be gone from the house together. Mackenzie had been back home from university for the winter months. They had taken a plane from Hammondville to Sydney and spent the weekend at a conference together.

Mackenzie remembered how she'd spent the entire weekend locked up in her bedroom, studying for the coming springtime exams. She had hardly thought to notice the alert which'd sounded on her Link; her parents letting her know that they had just got on the plane.

That they would be back home in a few hours.

To tell the truth, Mackenzie hadn't thought anything might be awry until she had surfaced from her studies, realised that more than six hours had gone by since she had heard from her parents, and that they should've been home by then.

It was soon after that she had received the phone call.

Once the funeral was over and done with, Mackenzie had taken the decision to drop out of university and to use her inheritance to go into business for herself.

She decided that—*at twenty*—she knew enough.

And, well, she'd mostly been proven right.

Her CV was testament to that.

An alert on the Link brought her attention back to reality with a snap.

She blinked several times, clearing the past from her vision.

Here she was. On the Moon.

Surely not even her parents could've realised *this* would be possible?

She jabbed a finger into her inner earpiece, watched on as the options flickered by her left eye. She flipped onto the messages she'd currently received. Saw that something had come to her from Entry Clearance. That her input was required.

The message was vague—obviously kept *deliberately* vague.

Throughout her years of management experience, Mackenzie had noticed that it was a well-worn tactic of inferiors to deliberately keep their reports vague in the hope that it would attract attention.

That she would want to know more.

In Mackenzie's opinion, this was something of a false dichotomy since she nearly always pushed such messages to the bottom of her action pile. She had *enough* details to pile through that she really didn't need *enigmatic* messages on top of that.

She decided that deletion was the best option with such messages. She had learned that if she decided against responding to any given message, the problem would either go away or—in the rare case that it was urgent—the person would write again. And with the proper details.

However, right as Mackenzie was on the point of eliminating the message, there was something which caught her eye. Or, to be more exact, it was a *name* which caught her eye.

Gofreddo Zito.

All at the same time, her heart gave a kick and her stomach sank.

It seemed that—ever since he had arrived—Gofreddo Zito had been causing some sort of a stir or other.

Whether it was the shitstorm she'd had to deal with surrounding his grandmother—and her burial at the Lunar One Monument—or his apparent negligence surrounding his 'job' working as a Lunar Shuttle pilot. Wherever Gofreddo Zito was, trouble was sure to follow.

But that didn't mean she could put him off.

Whether she liked it or not, Gofreddo was a dominant influence on the Moon; if only because of who his father was.

Even on her second run through, Mackenzie found it difficult to garner much in the way of content from the message. That this particular complaint involved some nonspecific 'package'.

She looked out over the landscape of the Celestial Stays Dome and then blew out another sigh.

Well, she couldn't put this off forever . . .

Charlie Cuevo—Mackenzie's personal assistant—looked particularly pleased to see her.

Whenever Mackenzie laid eyes on Charlie, she couldn't help but think just how devastatingly beautiful she was; what with her sleek, black, shoulder-length hair, and her nutty, chocolate-textured eyes. She had a good ten years on Mackenzie, too. She had the whole of her twenties all spread out before her while Mackenzie had already plunged into her early thirties—sometimes she couldn't help but think that life just wasn't fair.

The flag just below Charlie's nametag revealed her to be from Chile.

And—as Mackenzie knew from her encyclopaedic knowledge of her underlings—Charlie's hometown was Valparaiso.

As the two of them walked through Entry Clearance, past all the stations currently processing new arrivals, Charlie brought Mackenzie up to speed on what was currently taking place. It was just as she had outlined in the message: a strange package had arrived. It had come along on the latest Shuttle from Earth. Although it was standard procedure for all packages arriving to the Moon to be broadcast ahead of time—for their contents to be made public when they were loaded—this particular package hadn't had any of the standard tags associated with it.

And so Charlie had called Mackenzie.

They proceeded through a series of sliding doors, with Mackenzie wondering just what sort of a dilemma would be awaiting her now. Some days, she would freely admit, she would much rather have been back down on Earth. Some days she regretted having ever taken up the offer to become the Supervisor of Human Resources beneath the Celestial Stays Dome.

The room was strangely small. At least it *seemed* small when compared with the size of the package occupying much of the space.

Mackenzie glanced to Charlie, and then began to pace the circumference of the package. In many ways, it was much like any of the dozens of packages she had seen over the years in cartoons. It was wrapped in brown paper and seemed to be tied together with some sort of wrought string.

Once Mackenzie had made a lap of the package, she came to a halt, glanced to Charlie, and then said, "Let's open it up, shall we?"

It took the two of them tugging at the outer packaging—one on each side—to get shot of the paper.

And once they had done so, it was only to reveal the dull, grey box beneath.

Mackenzie gave what felt like her thousandth sigh that day.

She fixed Charlie with an arched eyebrow. "What'd you reckon?"

Charlie just gave a shrug by way of response.

Of course, protocol stated that only the person who was named as the recipient of the package could *officially* open it . . . however, in the absence of any sort of customs procedure, it fell to Mackenzie Angliss—and whoever she might choose to deputise for her—to decide whether or not it was prudent to search arriving goods.

"Let's open it up," Mackenzie said, finally.

Between the two of them, they worked at the flaps of the package, tearing it away where necessary. They'd already got about three quarters of the way through opening the package up when Mackenzie wondered if it wouldn't have been quicker for them to put some tool to work on the job. It didn't seem worthwhile now, though—now that they'd torn through the flaps and revealed what was inside. What *was* inside, was a great deal of protective packaging.

Between the two of them, Mackenzie and Charlie scooped their way through the foam and other packing materials. Before too long, Mackenzie found herself staring at the Chinese lettering on the side of yet another box. Although her Mandarin was hardly much beyond school level, she managed to decode that the contents had something to do with an inflight computer.

This confused Mackenzie for several seconds.

For one, Gofreddo had been stripped of his flying duties.

For another Celestial Stays received any supplies it required addressed to the appropriate department. Perhaps, in some cases, the package would be addressed for someone's attention, but never *wholly* for them. The concept of 'personal' deliveries was one which didn't really exist beneath the Dome. But, then again, this was Gofreddo Zito she was thinking about. And—as had already been established—Gofreddo Zito didn't play by the rules.

At least not the rules which *normal* people had to play by.

The rules which *Mackenzie* had to play by.

Charlie knew Mackenzie well enough not to pry or to ask questions about this device they had unwrapped. She simply stood at Mackenzie's shoulder, awaiting her next order.

"Go fetch Gofreddo, would you?" Mackenzie said.

Charlie remained fixed on the package before them for several seconds, and then, with a curt nod, set off to go and do her bidding.

As Mackenzie stood in the room alone, she realised that she had received another message. It was on the subject of Njhay and Louise's wedding. Unlike the nonspecific messages Mackenzie hardly had use for—like the one which Charlie had sent her about the package—this one was crisp and to the point. Mackenzie was required at a meeting a little later in the evening—at the Crescent Gardens—where they would go through the proposed running order for the ceremony.

Although Mackenzie couldn't help the twist in her gut, she also knew that her control freak self wouldn't allow Louise to sort everything out on her own. It was non-negotiable that—on Mackenzie's watch—everything needed to go off without a hitch . .

. she wasn't about to throw some *forgettable* wedding beneath the Celestial Stays Dome; the first wedding which would be held on the Moon. This was going to be—quite simply—the greatest wedding mankind had ever known . . . or at least the most *memorable.*

2

MATRIMONIAL DUTIES

ime had been running short, so Mackenzie had been forced to leave the suspicious package at Entry Clearance. In true, billionaire son's fashion, Gofreddo had been 'tied up' with something or other. Although on another day Mackenzie might've taken some sort of perverse pleasure in impounding Gofreddo's package, today she just found it one more administrative annoyance she could do without. But, all the same, she filed the report, gave the details, laid out all the reasons for her decision, and then left the matter with Charlie.

When Mackenzie swooped down in her Personal Transporter —PEAR—and descended onto the landing strip outside the Crescent Gardens, she had to admit that she was feeling a touch weary. As she trod the gravel path of the Gardens, the Dome lights were dimming, already preparing for the night-time portion of the day-night cycle.

Because it seemed the natural way to go, she plodded through the laboratories first, but, finding them deserted, came out the other side, emerging into the Gardens themselves.

Although Mackenzie had never been much interested in botany back at school, she had to admit that there was something calming about being surrounded by the trees, and the flowers, and to see grass spread out before her. It sent her back to Earth.

Sent her *mind* back to Earth.

Although she would be back there in a little under three months, Mackenzie never would've believed that she would miss the wind in her hair so much; a chilly drizzle blowing up against her cheeks. The sound of a seagull cackling in the distance.

All those little details which she'd left Earthside.

Mackenzie had almost lost herself to recollection—to the Gardens as they sprouted up on all sides—when she heard someone calling to her.

"Yoo-hoo! Over *here!*"

Mackenzie glanced up.

She narrowed her eyes, frowned.

Trying her best to see who had spoken.

She could make out nothing but foliage.

And then something twitched in the back of her brain.

Suddenly she saw them . . . the *group*.

They were all clustered beneath one of the few trees which Mackenzie actually did recognise. In truth, the only reason she really did recognise it was because of a school project she'd done when she'd been seven or eight years old. It was a red ash—a *Leather Jacket* as she recalled from the report she'd finally put together.

Once Mackenzie had spotted the group, she was able to recognise the person who had spoken:

Louise. Louise Williams.

The one who was getting married.

She took in her neat, blond hair which hung down to her shoulders, and the girlish, fragile structure of her cheekbones. Among the group, she also took in Njhay Garcia—Louise's betrothed. Although Mackenzie and Njhay had had their conflicts in the past, she couldn't help admitting that there was a *certain* handsome quality to Njhay; something which was *alluring* even.

Then there was Lan Niu, a member of the Security Division with her long, plaited, jet-black hair.

And then there was Lan's beau, Patrick Fourie, a Shuttle pilot; with his strawberry-blond hair. There was something about Patrick's stance which had occurred ever since he had begun to 'go out' with Lan . . . something about how he stood with a straighter back. It made his chin jut out just a touch more proudly, or so Mackenzie thought.

Mackenzie took in others among them.

Kyra Singh—editor of *Lunar Landings*. Her rich, hazelnut eyes, and the hair neatly coiled about her scalp. Then there was Julius Denisov, in charge of the Stellar Tide Cultural Centre. He had classical Slavic features, and cool, discerning eyes.

Alicia Brennan was there too. She wore a pixie-cut hairstyle and her rosy cheeks seemed to gleam even in the relative darkness of the Crescent Gardens.

There was thankfully no sign of her boyfriend, Gofreddo Zito.

That at least made Mackenzie feel a little better.

At least there was one other person who wasn't present in their couple.

Despite Mackenzie's best attempts to keep her personal life out of the brutal rumour mill which operated beneath the Celestial Stays Dome, she knew that her love life was freely discussed by all and sundry. That was one of the penalties for being so visible.

Besides that, she hadn't wanted to have a fuss kicked up with Gofreddo over that package of his which she'd been forced to impound. When Mackenzie met Alicia's eye, she couldn't help but expect her to ask her about it . . . to have Alicia *question* what she'd done. Alicia herself was a Supervisor, and clearly not frightened away from asking what she felt compelled to ask.

Mackenzie pressed on a smile.

She had assumed that Alicia might bring along a few others to this meeting.

Maybe some of those lower down on the totem pole.

The actual hands which would be working the catering, for instance. Or those from Hospitality who would be taking charge of the decorating.

Despite Louise and Njhay being—for want of a better word—her *friends*, Mackenzie was well aware that she needed to avoid her personal feelings getting in the way of her resource management. She wouldn't allow the clientele's lunar experience to be compromise in any way simply because the wants and whims of employees needed to be accommodated—it was part of the contract she had signed . . . it was part of the contract they had *all* signed.

The mood among the group was light-hearted, although Mackenzie felt herself becoming a little uneasy. She had never been at her best when it came to socialising—to having *friends*. Since her work had always been personal connections, and how best to manipulate them for profit, having friends had never seemed like something she could allow herself to enjoy.

"Mackenzie," Louise finally said. "We've got something we'd like to share with you."

"What?" Mackenzie replied, feeling her voice quiver slightly.

It annoyed her when she couldn't keep control of every aspect of her image.

When she could feel the mask she presented to the world slipping.

Louise glanced across the assembled group to Alicia.

"Actually," Alicia said, "it's probably better if we just *showed* you."

" 'Showed' me *what?*"

But the rest of the group just smiled back at her.

Not wanting to tell her anything.

3

SECRETIVE DEVICES

lthough Mackenzie's reflex was to tell the others that they really shouldn't bother with the secrecy—that, if they realised it or not, Mackenzie had eyes on everything that went on beneath the Celestial Stays Dome. It was her responsibility, as Supervisor of Human Resources, to know all that she could about her staff and clients.

But she managed to switch off that part of herself for the time being.

Maybe she was getting better.

Perhaps she'd be able to purge her control-freak nature yet . . . not that she really wanted to; it *had* proven to be an extremely valuable tool in her career thus far.

They boarded a fleet of PEARs, and immediately set off for the Shuttle Hangar.

Mackenzie was uneasy about the ride. She was worried that the others might be about to force her into doing something which was illegal. Or something which Celestial Stays specifically prohibited. It bothered her despite the fact that she could claim to be—in some way—the boss of most of those present here. She had to admit that peer pressure had a knack of acting more efficiently on her than she would've liked to believe. She liked to think that she could resist anything anybody tried on her—in a group or as individuals . . . but that wasn't quite the truth.

When they got to the Shuttle Hangar, the whole place was deserted.

All the Shuttles were lined up in a neat row, their wings tucked into their storage position. When Mackenzie glanced up, she realised that Patrick Fourie was giving her a worried look, as if she might be about to castigate him for one of the Shuttles being 'improperly parked' or something similar. However—to Mackenzie's untrained eye—the Shuttles looked as orderly as they could reasonably be expected to be.

Mackenzie fell into stride alongside Alicia, who appeared to know which way to go.

"This is top-secret," she said, turning her head to Mackenzie.

"Uh . . . right," Mackenzie replied, not quite able to keep herself from admitting that she had no idea what was going on here. She felt as if—in some way—she had failed in her role . . . as if she had somehow allowed an aspect of the Dome to sneak by her.

Most likely she was just being melodramatic.

Or perhaps she *was* losing her edge.

Mackenzie shifted a glance back over her shoulder to the others, noticing that Lan Niu hung back, at the Shuttle Hangar doors. She wondered if this was some sort of extra security—so that nobody would happen upon them while they did this 'top-secret' stuff.

They ventured across the floor of the Shuttle Hangar and then into what Mackenzie soon saw was the locker room . . . at least she was able to make this jump of logic from the various, off-white flight suits which hung off pegs, and that general, musky, sweaty smell of men which seemed to hang about in *all* locker rooms; on the Moon or back on Earth.

Alicia looped her arm through Mackenzie's.

This simple, girlish gesture took Mackenzie off guard for a few moments.

She and Alicia had certainly had their disagreements, and despite them now being Supervisors—the two of them theoretically, at least, being on equal terms—she wasn't quite there to feeling comfortable in her company. It was her own issue, though, Mackenzie decided.

Perhaps she'd just never been good at being a *girly-girl* . . .

The last person—Kyra—filed into the locker room and brought the door shut behind her.

Mackenzie wondered if this wasn't going to be some kind of an elaborate, unfunny windup.

Maybe all of these people had been plotting against her in secret for a long time; wanting to find a way to *embarrass* her. From the outside, Mackenzie could see how it might seem humorous to 'put one over' on the ever-serious Mackenzie Angliss.

To show everyone that she wasn't as powerful as she made out.

However, if there was a joke coming, then it was certainly being delayed as long as to make it uncomfortable.

Alicia glanced about them, as if checking to see if someone might've tagged along with the group—as if someone *uninvited* might've managed to get in on this meeting.

Because she couldn't help herself, Mackenzie said, "We're not going to do anything *illegal* here, are we?"

Again, the smiling faces.

Those *knowing* smiling faces.

For the first time, Mackenzie realised what it was like to not know the entire lowdown.

To not be acquainted with the full set of facts.

Alicia leaned into Mackenzie then winked. "Don't worry," she said. "Frau Köhler has cleared the programme herself."

"What 'programme' ?" Mackenzie said, deciding that now she might as well make her ignorance known . . . there didn't seem to be any benefit in hiding it.

Alicia cracked a wider smile now. "The *Zito* Programme."

It was Louise who unveiled the loose floor tile in the locker room which concealed a circular tunnel leading directly downward. And Louise was the one who led the way, clambering down the rungs of the ladder and into the darkness below.

"You're next," Alicia said to Mackenzie, with a smile.

Still not quite sure about what she had let herself in for, Mackenzie bent at the knees, looked over the group another time, and then descended into the hole.

When she set foot on the first rung, Alicia spoke up.

"Take care not to go too fast," she said. "It'd be a long way to drop if you slip."

Mackenzie did as she was told, continuing to descend the ladder.

She was surprised when she set foot on the concrete floor at the bottom.

The darkness was overwhelming.

Even as she stood there, she couldn't help but think about the Health and Safety implications. It was true to say that there was much about this place which might catch the attention of an overzealous Supervisor . . . just like her.

When she felt someone touch her in the darkness, she near enough leaped clean out of her skin. Apparently noticing her extreme reaction, Louise said, "It's okay—it's just *me.*"

Mackenzie composed herself. She tried to explain this away within her own head, telling herself that she hadn't *really* been taken off guard. It'd only been a matter of the circumstances. Of her being whisked away like this by the others. Of her sinking down into this dark, dank place.

She turned her attention upward, to the ladder which she had just come down.

And which the others were now descending.

She made out the circle of light marking the entrance to the manhole.

Then she glanced about, as if she might be able to make some sort of sense out of the darkness which surrounded her on all sides.

Quite against Mackenzie's expectations, Louise took her hand.

It wasn't often that people had the tenacity to touch her.

She supposed it was part and parcel of the all-round fear which she projected to the wider world; that sense of *fearful* respect she managed to elicit in others.

"This way," Louise said, a smile in her voice. "Come on."

With a final glance back at the ladder, and at Alicia, and the others, following her, Mackenzie allowed Louise to lead her deeper into the darkness.

There was a point when Mackenzie tried to divine just how high the ceiling of this enclosure actually was. Although she restrained the urge to reach out and touch the ceiling, she spent a good deal of time attempting to work out just how far the darkness above her head went on.

Finally, though, her imaginings proved to be all for nothing because a light blinked on.

It was one of those lights which didn't merely push back the dark, but which crushed it forevermore.

Mackenzie stood and absorbed her newly lit surroundings, unsure quite what to make of this.

Strangely enough, the first thing which struck Mackenzie was how *tall* this space actually was. It was nothing less than the same approximate capacity as a warehouse. She couldn't help thinking that it would make a great space for some element of Celestial Stays Hospitality . . . just what it could be put to use for, Mackenzie hadn't yet decided.

Once she had got over the room itself, she soon took stock of what stood in-between them; impossible to miss.

A spaceship.

She blinked several times, unsure quite what to make of this.

The spaceship was very different to the Shuttles in design— either the lunar Shuttles which ran across the plains; or the Shuttles which carried people up from the Earth and then back again.

Whereas the Shuttles were sort of a shoebox shape with a cockpit and a trio of wings jutting out, the spaceship before her was far more substantial.

To begin with, it was the shape of a stack of tyres.

As it grew taller and taller, the tyres grew smaller and smaller.

There was something distinctively *alien* about the whole ship . . . though Mackenzie supposed it was mostly because she still had that childlike image of alien craft resembling 'flying saucers'.

Mackenzie turned to Louise, awaiting her explanation, only to have something else catch the corner of her eye. She shifted her attention back front and centre, to the ship, and then to the platform alongside—set in a spotlight—where the figure stood.

Of course, Mackenzie soon enough recognised who it was.

Gofreddo Zito.

He stood up proudly, his arms folded over his chest.

He wore a slight smirk.

Mackenzie felt her stomach clench.

There was something about arrogance which had never sat well with her, but, it seemed, Alicia Brennan didn't have all that much trouble with it . . . at least for long enough to *take advantage* of Gofreddo's—admittedly—sculpted body.

Mackenzie just about had the presence of mind to realise that the others—Alicia, Njhay, Kyra, Julius, Patrick—had all come down the ladder. When she looked to the ladder, it seemed almost impossibly far away.

"Welcome!" Gofreddo Zito declared.

His voice boomed about the area.

And it sent a skitter up her spine.

Whatever she thought about Gofreddo Zito, there was no denying that he had the same 'presence' which his father possessed. The same power which allowed him to dominate any given room on the planet—or *off* it, for that matter.

Mackenzie caught hold of herself, straightening up and pressing on a more measured expression. "Well, this place is certainly impressive," she said.

It unnerved her somewhat that Gofreddo remained standing up on the platform; that he continued to look down on them. It put her in mind of some sort of a religious figure standing on a hill and addressing his followers.

Gofreddo only smiled wider. "We have Frau Köhler to thank

for that," he said. "For her kindness, and her *interest* in this very special project."

"Louise here said it was a *programme*."

Thankfully Gofreddo descended the platform. It felt as if they were nearer to being on a level playing field now that he was no longer raised above her. Although Mackenzie had never much believed in the *mental* aspect of business—of negotiation—she had to admit that, at times, she allowed herself to be taken advantage of by its cheap tricks.

"Yes," Gofreddo replied, still grinning from ear to ear. He stopped just before Mackenzie, looked her in the eye, as if he was examining her for some detail or other. Appearing to find it—or not—he broke off his intense stare. "We decided the time was right to bring you here . . . to *invite* you formally."

Mackenzie felt her chest tighten.

She looked about the others.

This was *so* strange.

Just about the strangest thing which had ever happened to her.

And that included the notion that it might be 'interesting' for her to accept a job on the Moon . . .

She pressed on her familiar business manner. "Invite me formally to what?"

Gofreddo's smile faltered. He bowed his head. Seemed to cast a stare off at Alicia.

Mackenzie wondered if bringing her here had been Gofreddo's idea at all. She wondered if that subtle glance might not be some unspoken request for confirmation that Mackenzie *really should* have been brought here. Finally, though, Gofreddo turned back to Mackenzie. "How'd you feel about exploring the stars—about leaving humanity behind? About advancing mankind's cause?"

Mackenzie had to admit that she was taken off guard by the question.

She looked about the others as if they could help her out with her own opinion.

They all looked at her with expressions of combined excitement and nervous anticipation.

For some reason, even though Mackenzie had guarded herself against such urges—or *thought* she had done—she couldn't help but feel herself *not* wanting to disappoint the crowd.

But, then again, this *was* a somewhat enormous question.

She turned back to Gofreddo.

"Hold up," she said. "Do you mind starting from, you know, the beginning?"

Gofreddo smiled widely, as if Mackenzie had already accepted his proposal. "What I am telling you is nothing short of my deepest, darkest dream."

The irony laced into Gofreddo's statement wasn't lost on Mackenzie.

Gofreddo continued, "As you are well aware—as the *whole* world is now aware—my grandfather was among those who were killed in the Lunar One Tragedy. One of those who perished during the first attempt to colonise the Moon."

Mackenzie *certainly was* aware of this.

She could still recall the enormous amount of media calls she'd had to field when the Zitos had decided that it would be a 'romantic' gesture for Gofreddo's grandmother to be buried alongside her husband. From what she had heard, Gofreddo had only found out about his grandfather's involvement in the tragedy relatively recently. Just why someone would decide to hide such information of a *noble* death from their family escaped Mackenzie.

Then again, since Mackenzie had heard about her parents' death at such an early age, she supposed that it had dulled her emotionally to further losses.

Was that a positive or negative thing?

Like most things in life, it had its advantages and disadvantages.

"It is my ambition," Gofreddo continued, "to resume my grandfather's dreams—but I wish to go beyond . . . beyond the Solar System. The technology already exists." He flourished his arm in the direction of the spaceship behind him. "It is only the will, the financial backing, which we have lacked." He broke into a more brilliant smile. "And, of course, there is the *crew* to consider."

Mackenzie of course understood that it would be the Zitos who would be funding the venture; that such a project had been waiting years and years for someone to put up the money. And she also understood the implications of such a mission. "You mean, you want to take us off on some death voyage?"

She expected Gofreddo's smile to at least waver, but he showed no signs of being affected by this statement. In the end, he only gave a slight shrug of his shoulder. "That is a possibility," he said. "Although we shall do our best to minimise risks."

"But we'll never return to Earth?"

Gofreddo shook his head. "I am afraid not."

Mackenzie analysed where she stood right at the moment. She could only be honest with herself. When she'd got up this morning, she had never imagined—not for a second—that she would be on the receiving end of such a proposition.

Then again, she supposed that it was a good thing that—even

after all the time she'd spent up here—the Celestial Stays Dome still had the ability to surprise her.

She decided to cut through Gofreddo's pitch.

To get down to the basic give-and-take of the thing.

"Why'd you want a killjoy like me on-board?"

Gofreddo laughed briefly.

Mackenzie couldn't help noticing that the others behind her chuckled along nervously.

She still held power over most of them, after all.

She was still—*officially*—their boss.

Even though Gofreddo was, in some ways, the most junior Celestial Stays employee among them, he had no reason to fear Mackenzie's wrath. Unlike the others, she wouldn't be the one to decide whether or not he would stay or go. To be quite frank, a decision such as that went far above Mackenzie's head.

Gofreddo met her eye with a new sense of sincerity. "We need someone who knows how to *manage* disparate aspects of the ship—"

"You mean you need someone to bust skulls?"

Gofreddo smiled warmly. He parted his lips, about to say something else. But then he gazed over the top of the others. When Mackenzie followed his eyes, she saw that he was looking at the ladder. Observing the pair of figures descending.

Mackenzie squinted, doing her best to make them out.

She could tell that the first person descending the ladder was Lan Niu—that made sense, seeing that she had been standing guard at the entrance to the Shuttle Hangar. The person behind her, taking far more care with his steps, was more obscure.

Mackenzie continued to stare at the pair, and Gofreddo continued.

"As far as the skull-busting goes, we already have someone for the job." He gestured to Lan, who had now landed on the concrete floor—leaving the ladder behind.

Mackenzie continued to analyse the pair of figures as they drew closer to the group—still trying, and failing, to make out the other one.

"No," Gofreddo continued, "we need someone who has a cool head for a crisis—who understands how people *knit* together." Here he demonstrated by threading his fingers into one another. "Someone who shall be able to guide the *ship.*"

"The captain?" Mackenzie asked, frowning.

Gofreddo made his lips pert. "I was thinking of something more along the terms of Flight Director."

" 'Flight Director' ?"

"Hmm," Gofreddo said. "It shall be your task to take all of the information at your disposal—all of the *human resources* at your disposal—and make the difficult decisions. Much as you have carried out the decisions here, beneath the Celestial Stays Dome."

Mackenzie's mind swirled.

Once again, she turned, took in the person who had just arrived to the group.

She recognised him now, of course.

His buzz-cut hair.

The tight muscles which rippled beneath his overalls.

And those quick eyes—nearly constantly on the move.

It was Miguel Cruz.

He was in charge of the Armstrong Archive.

An academic, learned man.

In many ways—Mackenzie supposed—he occupied the opposite end of the Celestial Stays spectrum.

As she took stock of him she felt her heart rattling at her throat.

Hadn't she noticed this before?

Hadn't she *seen* how attractive he was?

He caught her eye for the briefest of moments.

Mackenzie looked away.

And then she blushed.

God. What had she got herself in for now?

4

ENGAGING PROPOSITION

iguel had just about managed to get his head around this *place* . . . hidden beneath the Shuttle Hangar. And he was also getting used to the idea of the spaceship which was sitting right between them. He recognised it, of course.

About twenty, thirty years ago, there had been a spate of designs and all manner of prototypes for spaceships which might be capable of exploring the outer reaches of the universe.

The ship before him he recognised as a Sbrupta Six—so named because it was the sixth design which the Sbrupta design team settled on.

From what Miguel could recall from the story, the project had finally been abandoned because of a lack of funds . . . that familiar problem.

If there was one thing which had plagued the sciences—*and research in general*—through the ages it was a 'lack of funds'.

However, if there was one thing which Gofreddo Zito had in spades it was 'funds'.

Despite the group of people he stood among, and the fact that Gofreddo Zito was explaining in further detail how the mission would proceed—a mission which Miguel was *apparently* a part of! —he found his attention rendered somewhat distracted by another factor.

Although Miguel knew that she was a symbol of all that he hated—all that he was *supposed* to despise—he couldn't help but note just how fantastic Mackenzie looked today.

The gorgeous lustre to the red hair which flowed between her shoulders. And those fascinating, impossible-to-avoid green eyes which'd latched onto his for those insufficient moments. He snapped his attention back onto Gofreddo, realising that he was being asked a question.

"So," Gofreddo said, smiling—he was *always* smiling. "What would you make of being the ship's archivist?"

Although Miguel was certain this was the kind of decision which merited a great deal of Serious Thought, he couldn't help but feel himself swept up in the romance.

He might be floating out into space.

Away from the world.

Forever.

Right when he felt himself on the cusp of answering in the affirmative—short-circuiting the all-important period of profound reflection and consideration—Mackenzie leaped in.

"I think you'd need to give us a chance to consider."

Again, Miguel and Mackenzie's eyes crossed.

Miguel felt a fizzing, hot sensation pass through his blood.

He dragged himself back to Gofreddo.

Managed to find—from *somewhere*—a smile.

"Yes," he said, as if it was the most natural thing in the world, "I'd like some time to *think* this through."

Gofreddo threw up his hands, apparently in surrender, or maybe it was out of some sense of godlike patience. As if he couldn't quite believe that they were unable to make up their minds when the opportunity of a lifetime was offered to them.

And there was no mistaking that this *would* be the opportunity of a lifetime.

From what Gofreddo had explained, it would be Miguel's responsibility to archive and order a curriculum for the colony which they were setting out to found. He would be responsible for *generations* of children to come. His decisions would be the ones responsible for their perception of the Old World; for their perception of *Earth*.

The planet which they would never know.

They would *never* be able to visit.

Gofreddo clapped his hands together with a degree of finality, smiled again, and then gave a nod. "All righty—you just let me know when you've decided." And, with that, he turned his back on them, shifting his attention onto the spaceship.

Onto the Sbrupta Six.

Miguel's attention, though, had returned to Mackenzie Angliss.

5

CUSTOMS PROCEDURE

*M*ackenzie strode through *Entry Clearance.* Today she had a great deal on her mind. She wanted—more than anything—to just be able to slip off 'home' to the Basements. She thought about a quick session in the gym, and then a dip in the pool, followed by a long nap.

But there was no time for rest and relaxation.

Perhaps, if she did take up Gofreddo Zito's offer—to become the Flight Director on his mission into Outer Space—then she would have the time to let her hair down.

Then again, she wasn't entirely certain whether Gofreddo had thought to include something so *base* as entertainment and fitness facilities on that spaceship of his.

There was, of course, the subtext which'd accompanied the whole meeting.

The obvious fact that she and Miguel had been the only single-tons present.

She was certain that it was Gofreddo's intention for the two of them to couple up—just as the others had done . . . and then they'd trek out into space.

One great, big, loved-up family.

Ever since the meeting, Mackenzie had to admit that she'd begun to feel the need to resist. She'd felt the need to resist what she'd *felt* in Miguel's company. It had only been lust—that *most basic* of emotions. Throughout her time beneath the Celestial Stays Dome—throughout her life, in fact—she had lived by the credo that she should not get herself *emotionally involved* with anyone. And although she had enough self-awareness to know that this was most likely a direct result of her parents' death when she'd been younger—afraid of suffering through the same pain of loss again—she had decided that it was one of those eyes-wide-open decisions. It had kept her protected from some extremely bad business deals. The sorts of deals which might find themselves spoiled, in some way, by an inappropriately close personal relationship.

And—as Mackenzie had decided long ago—she would not allow *anything* to jeopardise her success. That included any role she might play on-board Gofreddo Zito's ship.

Then again, it seemed somewhat ridiculous that she was discussing this with herself.

Most likely, of course, there was nothing at all on Miguel's end.

It'd been a long time since Mackenzie had let anyone close.

Charlie showed up at Mackenzie's elbow presently. She had dark bags beneath her eyes and Mackenzie supposed she had been up for most of the night. That was one of the problems with being assigned to Entry Clearance—it was a twenty-four-hour job.

Once Charlie had brought her up to speed on all the latest goings-on, she was about to dismiss her when something occurred to her. Mackenzie stopped walking. "What happened to that shipment—the one addressed to Gofreddo Zito?"

"The inflight computer?" Charlie replied.

Mackenzie felt her stomach sink slightly. She thought back to how she had promised Gofreddo that she would keep this matter secret; that she would say *nothing* of the programme to anyone else, even if she did eventually decide against joining the crew.

She supposed that she had been *just a touch* brash in allowing Charlie to see so much of what the package to Gofreddo Zito contained. Perhaps on some level she had *wanted* Charlie to see what sort of liberties Gofreddo Zito took with Celestial Stays; what sorts of privileges were afforded him which would never be afforded other employees . . . maybe it had been her masterplan to kindle some sort of resentment in Charlie toward Gofreddo.

"I'd like to release it, from impounding," Mackenzie said, looking off over the people currently navigating Entry Clearance.

"Do you reckon he's building a spaceship?"

Although there was a smile clearly present in Mackenzie's voice, she couldn't help but feel a sudden rush of fury. By no fault of her own—or at least no *knowing* fault—Mackenzie had just gone and revealed the secret which Gofreddo had entrusted her with.

Realising that Charlie was looking to her for an answer—and that each second she failed to give one it came off as being more suspicious—Mackenzie said, "It's not our responsibility to question. Not our *place* to pry into client's details."

"But he's not a client—he's an employee."

Again, Mackenzie felt another rush of anger. This time she turned on Charlie with a severe glare. "You know what I mean. He's not an employee like us."

Charlie appeared to detect the sharp tone in Mackenzie's voice, and busied herself with some other task, jabbing her finger into her earpiece, checking on something or other.

Finally, apparently deciding that the tension in the air had slackened somewhat, Charlie said, "There have been rumours, you know?"

"This is the Celestial Stays Dome—there are *always* rumours."

"Yes," Charlie continued, "but these ones are *different* . . . there are those who say that Gofreddo plans to explore space. That he wishes to travel into the universe. That he is *searching* for people to be a part of his crew."

Although Mackenzie felt as if she was in danger of boiling over, she managed to hold herself back from losing control. In a way, she supposed that it was a nimble feat. She congratulated herself on not allowing her emotions to control who she was; who she projected to the world at large.

"I'd like to get the package out of impound later on today—do you think it would be possible?"

Charlie gave her a curt nod. "Certainly."

"Good," Mackenzie replied, and then walked away.

It was only when she got outside—when she left Entry Clearance behind to go about some other duty—that she realised she was trembling all over.

———

Standing in her office, Mackenzie was nearing the end of her shift when she finally decided that she needed to say something. Because she wasn't about to call Gofreddo Zito directly to her office, instead she settled on summoning Louise Williams and Alicia Brennan.

The two of them came right away—perhaps more testament to

their fear of Mackenzie than any sort of a reverence for protocol beneath the Celestial Stays Dome.

She explained the situation with Charlie as delicately as she could manage.

The two of them listened to her attentively.

When she was finished, Mackenzie felt strangely nervous.

Again, she made a point of not allowing herself to be one of those people who *got* nervous.

She much preferred to keep a steady hold on her emotions at all times.

Indeed, she *prized* that aspect of her reputation, even if she was the only one who fully appreciated it.

Louise and Alicia remained stern-faced for a long while before Alicia lightened the tone in the room, giving a smile, and then saying, "I propose that we adjourn to the Orbital Café."

Before Mackenzie could say anything more, Alicia and Louise were up and out of their chairs, and they were—*indeed*—headed for the Orbital Café.

They took a seat by one of the windows which looked out over the lunar plains.

Even though Mackenzie should've been used to the wonder of looking out over the lunar dust, she couldn't help but find herself becoming rendered hypnotised by the effect of the barren landscape. To think that this had once been a domain open only to dreamers and astronauts. A lot—*everything*—changed over time.

Mackenzie supposed it took a degree of perspective to understand that much.

If she did accept the place on Gofreddo Zito's crew then she would never see any of those changes ever again. Could she really give all that up?

Could she really give up her connection to Earth?

What did she have to tie her down—to stay behind for?

Oh, there was a long-ago seen second-cousin here, or a long-forgotten great-uncle there, but her parents were gone. She had no boyfriend. And certainly no husband or children.

Just what did she plan on doing back on Earth?

In some ways she supposed that once she finally got done with her lunar rotations—when she hit fifty years old, if she didn't grow tired of lunar life before then—there would be the uncomfortable prospect of growing used to life Earthside.

What would she do?

Travel?

But what kind of buzz could travel give her now that she'd left the Earth behind on multiple occasions? It would seem like a walk in the park by comparison.

She looked across the table, realising that one of the waiters was bringing a basket of something which smelled delicious. When Mackenzie got a look at what the basket contained, she saw that there was a selection of pastries:

Chelsea buns. Crumpets. English muffins.

On instinct, Mackenzie glanced across the table, catching Louise's eye.

Louise gave a shrug. "Sorry," she said. "Some habits die hard—guess the Old British Sweet Tooth is alive and well."

If there was one thing which she had always found consistent about the British it was their love of all things sweet. To be quite honest, Mackenzie couldn't blame them, what with the multitude of recipes which were on offer.

Mackenzie took one of the crumpets, somehow convincing herself that it was a 'healthy' option.

Well, it didn't *seem* to be packed with sugar—just a shame about the butter which was smeared all over it.

Once the waiter had retreated from their table and they had each been given a cup of black coffee to accompany their sweet treats, Alicia met Mackenzie's eye, smiled, and said, "You don't need to worry too much about this whole *top-secret* business, okay?"

Mackenzie was surprised to hear this. She slumped back in her seat, eyeing Alicia with no small degree of suspicion. "Why?" she asked.

Alicia shrugged. "We have to let out what's going on before too long—and it only makes sense that it should be sooner rather than later if people are already chatting about it." She cracked a wider smile. "As I'm sure you'll appreciate yourself, it pays to maintain the upper-hand when it comes to communication. Allows you to better stay *on-message*."

Mackenzie managed to summon a smile in response to Alicia.

Then she looked out of the window, to the lunar plains again.

Mackenzie breathed out, steaming up the glass as she did so. "How'd you two feel about this?" She eyed the horizon; the Earth creeping its way up above the curvature of the Moon. "I mean," she continued, "you'll never see Earth again."

There was a long pause. Either Louise and Alicia were giving this serious question the treatment it deserved or they were settling into their respective treats.

Mackenzie glanced back over them, seeing that neither had touched the treats or the cup of coffee.

It was Louise who spoke up first. "I guess I might feel differently if I wasn't going with the man I love—with the man I'm going to spend the rest of my life with."

Alicia seemed to consider Louise's response before saying, "Same here."

Mackenzie smiled back at them. "Then there's Lan, of course, she's shacked up with Patrick. And then Kyra and Julius. Don't you think this is, well, you know, a little beyond a leap of faith? What makes you all think that these relationships—that *your* relationships—will hold together?"

Both women gave Mackenzie an irritatingly *knowing* smile.

A pair of the smuggest grins Mackenzie had ever found herself on the receiving end of.

"You'll know when it happens," Alicia replied. "You'll know when you find the one."

Mackenzie continued to stare the two of them down. "All right," she said, "let's drop the bullshit, okay?"

Louise and Alicia exchanged glances.

"Are you—or are you *not*—trying to set me up with Miguel Cruz?"

For the longest time, neither Louise or Alicia said anything.

And then they burst out laughing.

6

STUDY PRIVILEGES

*M*iguel Cruz sat at his desk, located in the back room off the Armstrong Archive reception. He was currently poring over a physical book which discussed a great deal of the history involving the exploration of Outer Space.

In some ways, he found it heart-breaking, to go through these personal histories of the men and women involved in wishing to push back the frontiers of the known universe. These people, he decided, were much after his own heart. They found fulfilment in discovering the new—and not only in *discovering* but also in turning what was known in the past on its head; seeing things from a new angle.

It went without saying that it'd been almost impossible for him to shake the meeting with Gofreddo from his mind. Whenever he found a spare moment, he would turn his thoughts to whether or not he would accept the offer. It would be an *enormous* undertaking.

And one for which he might go down in history.

It made him smile—as he sat here, alone, in a near-deserted building on the Moon—to think about how he had always imagined himself going down in history as some sort of a quirky librarian figure. The man who overlooked the Armstrong Archive in its early days; the one who kept watch on the human history which was stored within these walls.

What a *noble* imprint he would leave!

It was strange, since he had never thought of himself as being ambitious.

In the neighbourhood where he had grown up—in Tijuana, Mexico—there had only been one important choice for him to make once he was through with school:

Callejeros or *Pardos*.

The Strays. Or the Browns.

Those were the two gangs which ran his hometown.

And his choice was clear-cut:

Choose one or get the hell out.

Miguel had lived alone with his sick mother for the entirety of his childhood. For as long as he could remember, it had only been the two of them. He had never met his father. And he had had no sort of extended family. Everyone else had left the neighbourhood behind.

He could still recall how he would have a book propped open in his lap while he sat up beside his mother; the two of them half-watching the TV while they paid their real attention to the gunshots and anguished screams in the street outside.

Often, he had thought of the prospect of getting his mother out of the city, but she required dialysis up to three times a week, and their insurance only covered the local hospital.

He had also thought of selling their house; of moving somewhere else . . . but when he had made the enquires all the estate agents had been wary of the neighbourhood and had never offered any sort of valuation which would allow such a dream to become reality.

No, Miguel had been stuck.

And there had been nothing for him to do.

For as long as he could remember, Miguel had attempted to steer clear of the gang members. This was a task which was far easily mentioned than accomplished, however, seeing that members of one or the other tended to hang out on every other street corner, their constantly searching eyes looking for some way of profiting; be it by burglary, or a mugging, or—with a longer-term goal in mind—the acquisition of a new member.

One night, however, Miguel had been carrying an armful of books back home from the library when a trio of the members of the *Callejeros* had stood in his path; prevented him from going any further; from returning home unscathed.

He had tried his best to sneak through a gap in their group, but one of them had seized hold of his shoulder and hurled him backward.

Somehow, Miguel had succeeded in staying on his feet.

And, even then, he had had enough courage to look each and every one of them in the eye.

When they had asked him where he was going, and what he had in his arms, he had told them honestly. There was little point in him playing some sort of game. He knew that these people were as violent as they were stupid. They would cut off his head and leave it on his mother's doorstep if they thought it would prove a point. It was then that they'd asked him—Miguel always remembered—if he was 'serious'. What they were really asking him, though, was whether or not he wanted to keep his head on his shoulders.

There had been no other option available, so he had allowed them to take him away. To steal him off into a side alley. Everything had happened so quickly from then on. He recalled how he had been shoved through a beaded curtain and into an overly hot front room. The air had been clammy with the stench of cooking rice, and of some spices he couldn't quite think to identify. He was too *panicked* to identify such details.

They had told him to take off his shirt.

To lie face down on the couch.

He had done as they'd said.

Then he'd waited.

He supposed that he had expected just about anything. He had wondered if they were going to decapitate him from behind. If they were going to bring a sword down on the back of his neck. It would be a swift death—or so he hoped. But, although there had been pain, it hadn't been with any sort of murderous intention. On the contrary, it appeared that they wanted him *alive*.

The pain was almost impossible to stand. He had let out several groans as he had slowly become accustomed to the prick of the needle. He had been able to smell the blood on the air before too long. It had been more than two hours when someone slapped him on the buttock and told him to 'come back tomorrow to finish' that he was finally allowed to leave.

Even at the time, he'd been glad that his library books had been returned to him.

Apparently unharmed.

His mother—thankfully, at that point—had been mostly oblivious to the world passing around her. She was on an assortment of painkillers. She hadn't noticed the plastic film which had covered his back, and the tattoo which'd been sketched upon his skin, and which would have its inking completed the following day . . . because if Miguel didn't return then it was as good as signing his own death warrant. And that was how he had got his start with the *Callejeros*.

But he had never progressed beyond the lower echelons.

He had gone along with everything which was expected of him —short of actually *killing* anyone—and then, when his mother had finally passed away, he had seized his moment.

Realised that it was his chance to escape the city, and the gangs.

He had studied hard, and he had done his best to cover the tattoo on his back, but he had suffered the inevitable run-ins . . . those moments when he couldn't manage to avoid conflict with the gang members. He had come out of those mostly unscathed.

That was thanks to his conditioning, to his single-minded ambition to stay in shape . . . and to always know how to fight his corner.

When he'd got through with his studies, and he'd come across the opportunity with Celestial Stays, it had seemed the only obvious choice to jet off the Earth and to start a new life on the Moon.

And so here he was.

In the Armstrong Archive.

Some kind of a ghetto academic.

And now he had the chance to go down in history.

And not just as some quirky librarian . . .

Then there was the woman he had seen in the Shuttle Hangar, when Gofreddo had brought them all together for the meeting.

Mackenzie Angliss.

Of course he knew who *she* was . . . and yet, she had always struck him as being out of reach.

But—not to put too finer point on this—the concept of them travelling into Outer Space together had changed everything.

They would be the only single members of the crew on board.

Something would have to happen.

Wouldn't it?

7

EARTHSIDE ADVICE

In her office at the Lunar Grand, Mackenzie prepared for her weekly meeting with Frau Karolin Köhler, the owner of Celestial Stays. Despite the fact that she had gone through with thousands of these meetings now—in the time she'd occupied the role of Supervisor of Human Resources—she still felt herself becoming nervous. Even though Frau Köhler was nothing if not friendly—as accommodating as a saint—Mackenzie could never quite bring herself to feel one-hundred-percent comfortable in her company.

Mackenzie accepted the video-link request from Earthside. And she found herself staring into Frau Köhler's eyes. As always, Frau Köhler wore a wide smile. Mackenzie felt her gut clench as she stared into her grey-white eyes. As she absorbed the jagged, bright-white wig she was currently wearing. Or was it an augmentation? If it was indeed a wig, then it looked so lifelike that Mackenzie had trouble seeing it as anything other than genuine human hair.

Frau Köhler was sat behind the desk in her Berlin office, the Brandenburg Gate over her shoulder. Since Frau Köhler's feet were stowed out of sight, beneath the desk, Mackenzie had no chance to get a glimpse at what sort of shoes Frau Köhler had on today.

She was a *little more* than moderately famous for her choice of footwear.

"How're you getting on?" Frau Köhler asked.

Unlike other people Mackenzie had worked with—the types of people who appeared to see greetings as nothing other than a necessary part of social-linguistic programming which were regurgitated more out of habit than nicety—it always sounded as if Frau Köhler *really was* concerned for Mackenzie's welfare . . . And this had, in turn, made it so that Mackenzie thought carefully about how she should answer the question. She always wanted to answer the question in the genuine spirit with which it had been asked.

With honesty.

Finally, she settled on, "I'm doing okay."

Frau Köhler arched an eyebrow.

Mackenzie couldn't help but smile. "All right," she said. "I'm sure that you of all people will know that Gofreddo put the proposition to me—he wants me to go along with him on his Voyage to the Stars, or whatever the hell he's got it into his mind to call it."

Mackenzie paused, scanning Frau Köhler's reaction.

She realised that Frau Köhler was waiting for her to say some more.

To be quite honest, though, Mackenzie knew almost nothing about the proposed mission; nothing beyond the vague claim that she would be the 'Flight Director' . . . and then she settled on a concern which *had* floated about her mind.

"It would be difficult to leave Celestial Stays behind," Mackenzie said. "I hope you appreciate that—I hope you *understand* that it's a real dilemma." She glanced up briefly, finding Frau Köhler's intense stare upon her. "And that's before I even get my head around the idea that I won't ever return to Earth . . . that I'll never see it *again.*"

This was one facet which had only recently come out—when she'd met with Louise and Alicia.

They had informed her that the ship would launch as soon as possible; and that they would head right away into Outer Space. There would be no time for tearful farewells to all those who Mackenzie might still know down on Earth.

There were very few of those who remained now.

While Mackenzie voiced her concerns, Frau Köhler remained silent, merely hearing her out. Waiting to see if there was anything she might be able to help with.

Why *did* Mackenzie feel uneasy in Frau Köhler's company?

She was more like a well-trusted friend than the superstar, billionaire CEO of their age . . .

Realising that she had nothing else to say—nothing else which came to mind, in any case—Mackenzie sat still and looked deeply into Frau Köhler's eyes.

Frau Köhler took this just as Mackenzie hoped she would; as the opportunity for her to voice her own thoughts on the subject.

"There's something else," Frau Köhler said. "Something you're not telling me."

Mackenzie felt a heat rush through her bloodstream.

Her heart pulsed at her temples.

Because there *was* something which she wasn't telling her.

How did Frau Köhler manage to *do* that?

"Well," Mackenzie began, beginning to feel her voice shake—

she supposed that Frau Köhler was among the few people alive who could actually succeed in making her feel well and truly nervous, "I have some doubts about the rest of the crew."

Frau Köhler said nothing in reply.

She only smiled.

And waited.

Mackenzie couldn't help but wonder if—in another life—Frau Köhler had been a therapist of some description. "It's . . . well," Mackenzie continued, "they're all, you know, *paired* off?"

Frau Köhler's smile widened.

Mackenzie knew there was no hope of her stopping right there. Frau Köhler would know, without a doubt, that she was holding something back.

What Mackenzie realised was that it really had nothing to do with the fact that she was trying to please a boss . . . that she was worried if she failed to tell her *absolutely everything* she would get into some sort of trouble. With Frau Köhler it was something very different.

Something *elemental.*

Just something in her makeup made people want to open up to her.

To be as honest as they could possibly be.

"As it stands," Mackenzie said, "there are four couples on board the ship . . . and then there are a pair of singletons." This time she couldn't quite bring herself to look Frau Köhler in the eye, whether or not she felt that they possessed a shared confidence. "Miguel Cruz, the man who works at the Armstrong Archive —and *me.*"

Finally, Mackenzie did look up.

And she met Frau Köhler's eye.

"Do you see what I mean?" Mackenzie finally found herself saying.

Frau Köhler looked on her with a kind of grandmotherly grace, then replied, "I suppose you're a bit worried—given your surroundings. You would be the only ones on-board who *wouldn't* be in a relationship. And that you might well be feeling a sort of pressure to—how should I put it?—*get together?*"

Mackenzie said nothing.

But it was obvious that Frau Köhler had struck the exact point of her preoccupation.

Mackenzie fiddled with her hands in her lap for a few moments. She realised that she hadn't fidgeted in such a way since she'd been a little girl. She looked up at Frau Köhler once again. "What would you advise?"

Frau Köhler stared long and hard at Mackenzie, and then, slowly and surely, she steepled her hands and leaned back in her desk chair. She peered over her arched knuckles, closed one eye, as if examining a precious stone. "Well, that all depends on what you think of the boy."

8

TENSE INTERFACING

*W*hen *Mackenzie got through* with the call to Frau Köhler—and she felt as if she had blushed a good proportion of her bloodstream into her cheeks—she set her mind to the business-end of things.

Once they had got through with all the talk about boys, Mackenzie had informed Frau Köhler about the current state of gossip; that it seemed as if the whole Dome was on the cusp of discovering just what Gofreddo Zito was up to.

It didn't quite surprise Mackenzie when Frau Köhler revealed that she already had an inkling that this was the situation—and Mackenzie suspected that she had already had some sort of dialogue with Gofreddo himself.

In the end, though, Frau Köhler was kind enough to humour Mackenzie—in allowing her to feel some *semblance* of control—by granting her the responsibility of how she would allow the information to permeate the Dome.

There was, of course, only one sensible way of going about

the task.

And that was what had brought her here—to the Armstrong Archive.

When Mackenzie had walked through the lobby, it had been half on her mind that she might run into Miguel Cruz. She had been trying her best to put that specific notion out of her mind since the meeting with Frau Köhler. Now, more than ever, she needed her wits about her; and there would be little chance indeed of making cool-headed decisions if she was running about like some hormone-crazed teenager.

This was forever.

She would *never* return to Earth.

There would be no backup plan.

She would simply be *gone*.

Once Mackenzie had navigated the Armstrong Archive lobby without running into Miguel Cruz, she had felt a strange mixture of emotions.

Prime among them, though, had been disappointment.

And although she did her best to cast off this feeling it continued to nag at her.

When Mackenzie reached the upper floors of the Armstrong Archive, she was immediately struck by the sense of constant frantic motion—people jostling through the corridors, others shouting at the tops of their voices, and more still tucked into nooks and crannies hunched over vidscreens, hard at work relaying their thoughts into some form of text.

In short, Mackenzie imagined that it was a scene which would've been familiar in just about any newsroom down on Earth ... only this one was up on the Moon.

Mackenzie was used to experiencing a certain sense of reverence whenever she chose to visit any given part of the Celestial

Stays Dome. Everyone seemed more than aware that she was Frau Köhler's eyes on the ground. Now, though, hardly anyone looked her in the face, let alone went out of their way to give her any sort of respect—whether merited or not.

Mackenzie had to admit that it was something of a refreshing change.

She had never trusted people who kissed the ground she walked upon.

Those sorts of people always had an agenda of some sort.

Mackenzie waded through the crowds which streamed through the corridors of *Lunar Landings*—the Moon's media outlet—and finally succeeded in identifying Kyra Singh, the editor, some way across the room.

Mackenzie also noted that Louise Williams was busily working away at something. She glanced up from her own vidscreen, gave Mackenzie a smile and a wave, and then returned to work.

As always seemed to be the way, Kyra was surrounded by a whole crowd of people.

A whole crowd of *reporters*.

Mackenzie had to admit that she was impressed. Kyra really had worked hard to grow *Lunar Landings* so that it would've been the envy of any Earthside newsroom. Although Mackenzie had certainly been sceptical at first, when Frau Köhler had claimed that she would give Kyra Singh total trust when it came to editorial content, Mackenzie couldn't comment except to admit that—as always seemed to be the case—Frau Köhler had made exactly the right call.

Whereas before it had always been Celestial Stays's modus operandi to drip news down to the Earthside media in the form of stilted press releases—much in the way that most other businesses ran—Kyra Singh's reports on Gofreddo Zito, and particularly the burial of his grandmother at the Lunar One Monument, had illustrated the thirst for the Earthside public to get a more *genuine* impression of all that happened beneath the Dome.

After her discovery—the fact that Kyra had been filing reports to media outlets down on Earth—Frau Köhler had opted against sending Kyra back down to Earth on the first Shuttle available, and instead granted Kyra Singh this role, as editor of *Lunar Landings*.

Although Mackenzie was nothing of a journalist herself, she could certainly recognise enough about business that Kyra was becoming an increasingly important voice in her profession; that the simple fact that she *ran* the only media outlet on the Moon lent her a certain prestige which wouldn't be afforded the run-of-the-mill media editor.

When Kyra met Mackenzie's eye, she gave her a smile.

Over the past few weeks—while Kyra had been finding her feet with *Lunar Landings*—the two of them had struck up something like a friendship.

Mackenzie supposed it was because they were both maligned in some way or another.

Kyra because of all those stories she'd leaked to Earth.

Mackenzie because she was almost always *someone's* boss.

Once Kyra had dismissed the last of the reporters with an ease which Mackenzie could only stand by and admire, Mackenzie trod up to her. When she noticed she was smiling, she realised that it was authentic contentment. Not just for appearance's sake.

"Looking busy today," Mackenzie said.

Kyra flashed her eyebrows. "Yeah, tell me about it—we've had a whole bunch of reports in from a team of scientists out on the plains. Think they might've found an additional source of water." She grinned widely, apparently unable to restrain showing off her glee at this scoop. "This will be the first really *meaty* story we've dealt with—you know, a real discovery."

"Well, if we end up shooting off with Gofreddo we'd better get used to discoveries. They'll come thick and fast, I imagine."

Kyra gestured to a quiet nook of the newsroom so the two of them could speak in relative peace. The nook had a small window with a spectacular view out over the Celestial Stays Dome. Mackenzie took in her surroundings for a moment, and then turned back to Kyra.

"I've come about the press release," Mackenzie said. "Well, I don't know *what* you'd call it exactly. I spoke with Frau Köhler— she wants to go public with the news about the mission as soon as Gofreddo gives it the okay."

"And you think he will?"

Kyra sounded surprised.

That took Mackenzie off guard.

Mackenzie felt a moment's doubt. "That was what Frau Köhler intimated to me. That was what *Alicia* told me. They both said that there's not much point in us keeping up the façade if it's already common knowledge. It's just like the reason you and Frau Köhler decided to put together *Lunar Landings*—to 'control the message', you know?"

Kyra considered this a second.

Then she glanced about the newsroom.

"This is big," she said.

"Yeah."

Kyra turned back to her. "No, I mean it's big, you know, for *us*?"

"In what way?"

"Well, I expect, if we do decide to go public with the mission then it wouldn't really serve any use to maintain secrecy as to the identity of the crew. The details would leak out anyway—things have a habit of going that way when there's a big announcement of this sort. Things are manic. *One* of us will let slip."

"And so what if the flight roster is known?"

Although Kyra shrugged and her body language seemed to indicate that she was somewhat nonplussed by this development, there was a certain swiftness to her eyes—how they swished about their sockets, constantly on the move, hoping to make some observation or other.

A breakthrough.

Finally she replied, "I think, in a way, it would lock us into the mission. It's not going to be easy to back out once our names have been written in stone."

Mackenzie smirked. "I don't reckon anything's been written in stone for a hundred years."

But when Kyra turned back to her, she didn't share her jovial expression.

In fact, she looked deadly serious.

"You know what I mean," she said.

9

EARTHSIDE CONCERN

*A*s *the sun set* behind the Brandenburg Gate, Karolin Köhler looked about her office.

It was strange to think that this would be the last time she would take in this sight.

But she had decided that now was the time.

Now was *her* time.

The past few months had been hectic. It had been no easy trick for her to make the transition from a cutthroat, profit-making enterprise to one which—for the most part—would be a force for good.

She understood when people said that their work was their life, but in her own case she would always go one step further. Celestial Stays, for her, was *far* more than her life . . . which was to say that she believed it would outlive her. There was really only one term for her to use in describing it:

Her legacy.

As always, her office was neat and tidy—perhaps even *immacu-*

late if she was being particularly self-congratulatory. It had always been something of a crusade of hers to make sure that she never knowingly inconvenienced another person. And it was with this desire that she had determined to keep things orderly in her office.

Once she was gone, it would be a simple case of cracking open the top drawer of her desk then looking over the itinerary she had left there.

For some reason, she still preferred the old ways.

The *written* word.

Scribbling away on paper.

There was a certain weight to a physical document.

A certain *gravity*.

With a sigh, she noted the empty, cardboard coffee cup she had bought earlier and then discarded in the bin by the door. She thought on this sight for a moment and then bent down and retrieved it from where it lay in the base.

It was better *not* to make work for anyone.

It was better for her to clean up her *own* messes.

Surprisingly, with the coffee cup in her hand, Karolin felt far more at ease, as if she had just made a breakthrough in some apparently unsolvable conundrum.

Yes, now she could go.

And have her peace of mind.

Without another moment's hesitation, she turned out the light.

And shut the door.

PUBLIC RELATIONS PROTOCOLS

s Mackenzie descended the staircase to the Armstrong Archive lobby, she couldn't help wondering if she hadn't only succeeded in multiplying her to-do list following the meeting with Kyra. The two of them had thrashed out the basics of how they would run the story about Zito's Quest to the Stars . . . this was a running title—*thankfully*—and Mackenzie hoped they would settle on something a little less . . . *tabloid*.

They had planned first to announce the news to the Celestial Stays employees, and then, later, to the clientele. Soon after, the first reports to Earth would run. They would publicise the list of the fledgling crew for the mission along with the particulars. According to Kyra, it was better to oversaturate the media with facts than to allow room for *misinterpretation*.

All that remained now was Gofreddo Zito's final sign-off.

He would tell them when.

When considering the deserted, almost stony coldness to the

Armstrong Archive lobby, it was odd to think that there was a nerve centre of such great activity—only a few floors up—with the *Lunar Landings* newsroom. Then again, Mackenzie supposed that there were countless buildings—in countless *cities*—around the world where a space devoid of life was located right beside one which was bristling with energy. *Vitality.*

She reached the bottom step of the staircase, and fixed her attention on the doorway which led out to the Armstrong Archive landing strip. She felt her heart ticking along normally. Her whole body felt strangely *calm.* It always felt that when she could talk about her problems they didn't seem so insurmountable after all. And she had lots of support—wherever she looked, actually.

All she had to do was *ask.*

Right as she was eyeing the PEAR currently descending on the landing strip—and daydreaming about a quick swim before bed in the Basements—she heard someone speak from off to her side.

To begin with, Mackenzie felt slightly dopey, as she always did when she'd vexed her brain somewhat. However, when she saw who it was—when she saw *who* stood behind the reception desk— she regained her freshness.

It was Miguel.

Miguel Cruz.

As she studied him, she couldn't help but trace that tattoo which snaked out from beneath the collar of his overalls. And absorb how it seemed almost at odds with the glasses he currently wore.

She had to admit that she hadn't seen him with glasses before .. . and she also had to admit that they *suited* him quite nicely . . .

"Burning the midnight oil?" Mackenzie asked.

It was only after she'd spoken the question that she realised she had no idea what time it actually was. She didn't work to a shift like the majority of the Celestial Stays staff.

In fact, she liked to give the impression that she didn't sleep at *all*.

Apparently realising that she had been staring at his glasses, Miguel blushed slightly and reached up for them. He slipped them down his nose, folded them shut, and then dropped them neatly into the breast pocket of his overalls.

"Something like that," he finally replied.

Mackenzie felt a weird *heat* pass through her blood. Of course, she could still recall that feeling she'd had in the Shuttle Hangar, when they'd been giving Gofreddo Zito's ship a once-over.

She had been *attracted* to him.

Hell, looking at *that* hard chest—*that* ripped abdomen—she had no trouble admitting, if only to herself, that she was attracted to him *now*. It required more strength than she had anticipated merely to take a few steps toward him. He certainly held *some* kind of power over her. Feeling that she stood at a comfortable distance, she said, "Had any more thoughts about the mission?"

Miguel shrugged. "Not really—how about you?"

"To be honest, it's pretty much the only thing I've been thinking about."

Miguel blushed a little deeper now. He bowed his head, smiled. "Actually, it's the same for me." When he brought his head back up, his eyes—his *handsome* eyes—caught hers for no more than a moment. "I guess it's what you'd call a life-changing decision, huh?"

"Tell me about it."

The two of them slipped into an uneasy silence.

More than anything, Mackenzie wanted to make some light-hearted quip.

She wanted to put a smile on both their faces.

But 'light-hearted quips' were something which she'd never been all that good at.

Instead, she just looked him in the eye, and said, "I get the feeling that the others are trying to set us up. Don't you?"

Miguel's eyes widened. His lips turned slightly at the corners as he gave a bemused smile. "I . . . uh . . . I wouldn't . . ."

And then, because it seemed the right thing to do, she laid her palm flat on the reception desk and then lurched over the desk itself, crushing her lips against Miguel's.

To begin with, he held back, apparently unwilling to commit himself. But then he met her strength—pushed *back*. She felt his smooth, careful tongue tracing the line of her bottom lip.

A playful nibble.

At first there was a tingle in her gut. And then it became an outright *throb*.

Before she knew it, Mackenzie felt as if her blood had caught fire.

She felt as if the blood which now pumped around her system *lit her up*.

Not that she minded, of course.

She finally drew back from the kiss, holding her eyes shut for the longest time. When she opened them, she realised that Miguel had had his eyes shut too.

Between them, they laughed nervously.

A dry—*unsure*—laugh.

As Mackenzie turned to head out of the Archive, and toward the landing strip, she couldn't help getting in the last word. "I reckon they're barking up the wrong tree—trying to get us together."

But, as she left Miguel—no doubt—open-mouthed and struggling to work out just what had happened, she couldn't keep the smile from sneaking onto her lips.

Perhaps this *was* more than lust.

Time would tell.

11

RECOVERY POSITION

*M*iguel *stared at the spot* where he had last seen Mackenzie for a long moment.

He was paralysed.

His whole body felt as if it'd been *frozen* by her mere presence.

Let alone her kiss . . .

The tingling just wouldn't stop—it travelled the length and breadth of his body. He blinked himself free of his daze and returned to the back room, where he had been reading through yet more of the material on Outer Space exploration.

He sat in the chair and began to flip through the pages, but he soon realised that he was going to have extreme difficulty getting beyond the surface sense of the words. It seemed that he needed to reread each word seven or eight times . . . and *still* it didn't lodge in his brain.

Feeling overcooked, he rose to his feet and paced back and forth.

This was a *real* dilemma.

A *real* dilemma.

Throughout his life, he had liked to think that he *always* made decisions based on logical thought processes. He left very little to his gut. Perhaps it was because that was how academia worked . . . at least when it came to *archives*. There had to be systems and procedures for everything. There had to be *evidence* to back up each action taken.

But *just how* could he reason away his wanting to head off on this quest into Outer Space when all the reading he'd done on the subject pointed to the inarguable truth that it was an endeavour fraught with unnecessary danger?

Finally feeling as though he had managed to get himself back under control—at least his heartrate was beating nowhere near as quickly as it had been previously—he returned his attention to the current book he had been leafing through.

It was impossible for him to deny what it was that he had read there; and the conclusions which had been drawn book after book after *book*.

To put it into blunt, no-nonsense terms, all of the research on the subject of manned space exploration and colonisation pointed to the conclusion that it was at best foolish and at worst tragic. Considering the current status of robotic systems—of *droids*—it had been argued time and time again throughout the many books Miguel had read that it would be infinitely more practical to put *machines* to such a task.

To begin with, there was the whole issue with the selection of the crew—of gathering those who would fit psychological profiles. These people would be living the rest of their lives together in a confined space. This wasn't a problem which an unmanned ship would have to deal with.

Next—assuming that whoever managed the mission could find

compatible crewmembers—there was the matter of keeping the human beings alive. Of taking care of their day-to-day needs for the rest of their lives. Perhaps this was a lesser problem from Gofreddo Zito's point of view seeing that it could be taken care of with money. Medical care, for example, would be taken care of by the on-board droids. But, to Miguel's mind at least manned space exploration seemed nothing but a vanity project; and one which would—*very likely*—cost the lives of all those who signed up for it. That said, Miguel couldn't help but return to the romance of the whole idea.

The fact that he would be responsible for the next generation.

It would be up to *him* to provide them with a balanced education.

He would form their worldview.

For the crew, he would act as something like a gateway into the entirety of human knowledge. Sort of like a user-friendly interface for an unknowably vast database.

And the gravity of this role wasn't lost on him.

Feeling as though he had just about got a hold on his senses—that he was beginning to *boil down* following his 'encounter' with Mackenzie—he slumped in the desk chair, slipped his glasses free of the breast pocket of his overalls, propped them on the tip of his nose, and then resumed his reading. He scanned the next few paragraphs, and then, deciding that he wasn't going to find any new information which would alter his logical conclusion, he slammed the book shut.

Why was this such a difficult problem when the solution stared him so obviously in the face?

Perhaps he was far more affected by the world—by its *rawer* aspects—than he had ever wanted to believe.

Maybe he was more *human* than he had anticipated.

12

MATERIAL ACQUISITION

*S*at in the *PEAR beside Charlie,* Mackenzie descended to the Lunar Grand.

Between the two of them they bore a zipped-up plastic bag which put Mackenzie in mind of a body bag; those coverings they used to transport dead bodies. However, she knew that this particular bag didn't contain anything so grim as a deceased human being.

It was Louise Williams's wedding dress.

They hopped out of the PEAR and trod into the Lunar Grand.

Using the Link—sticking her finger into her inner ear—Mackenzie was able to fathom Louise and Alicia's location. When they came across the room, she realised that it wasn't only Louise and Alicia who were present, but that Kyra and Lan were there too.

Mackenzie looked about their faces, and couldn't help but feel a touch *uneasy* about them being here. She had expected to find herself alone with Louise and Alicia. Indeed, she felt far more *comfortable* in their presence—and *their* presence alone.

Alicia had already set up the room so that the wallpaper had transformed into a mirror. It showed off the reflections from all angles. When Mackenzie caught sight of herself, she couldn't help but wonder if she hadn't gained a kilo or two over the past few weeks.

Maybe it was just the *bend* of the glass . . .

There was a dressmaker's dummy in the centre of the room and Alicia slipped the plastic bag containing the wedding dress free of Mackenzie's grip, as if she might be of a mind to do it some damage, whether consciously or subconsciously.

To be quite honest, Mackenzie couldn't help but feel that Alicia was only being sensible in commandeering the wedding dress from her possession. Despite her outward appearance of being tidy and organised, she had always believed that she was something of a *klutz* . . . it seemed almost inevitable that if there was something to be knocked over she would be the one *to* knock it over.

As she stood awkwardly to one side, she watched on as Alicia unzipped the bag and removed the dress from within.

Mackenzie really knew next to nothing about dresses themselves, and she knew even less about *wedding* dresses. It was white, that much she could tell, and there was an assortment of precious stones attached to the garment. It was a scooped neck, with a flowery hem . . . and that was about where her expertise on the subject came to an end.

Alicia set about placing it on the dressmaker's dummy, made a few minor adjustments—although Mackenzie really couldn't tell what they were—and then stood back as if to admire the garment properly for the first time.

Mackenzie glanced to Louise, on the other side of the room.

She was going to be the *bride*, after all.

She was taken somewhat off guard by the fact that she wasn't smiling.

Was she ... *frowning?*

Mackenzie looked to Lan and then to Kyra, as if to check whether or not they'd noticed Louise's reaction. Then she turned to Charlie, who'd come in with her, who met her eye briefly. *Charlie* had noticed Louise's reaction—that much was certain.

Deciding that she might as well take a chance on killing the enthusiasm in the room, Mackenzie addressed Louise when she said, "Is everything all right?"

Louise remained very still—her gaze fixed on the dressmaker's dummy, and the wedding dress which hung down off it. Several times, she parted her lips as if to speak, but then said nothing at all. Finally, everyone in the room turned their attention onto Louise.

Mackenzie couldn't help thinking if she hadn't made a big mistake in calling everyone to *look* at her. If Louise truly was suffering from some sort of private 'anguish' then it wasn't like it was Mackenzie's place to highlight it.

But now it was too late.

"Louise?" Alicia said, turning away from the dummy.

Louise took one look at Alicia and then looked to Mackenzie.

It was a single movement.

Louise clutched her hands to her face and—lost in sobs—rushed from the room.

All of them listened as Louise's footsteps disappeared away off down the corridor.

Then a silence descended over all of them.

Mackenzie felt her stomach clench tight.

Lightning danced about her veins.

It was Kyra who finally spoke. "So, do you think she likes the dress?"

Mackenzie didn't take more than a moment to appreciate this witticism before she turned on her heel and headed out of the room. After Louise.

At first, Mackenzie was at a loss in her pursuit of Louise. She checked all the usual places—which generally meant the nearest ladies' toilets—but she couldn't track her down.

She thought about returning to the room, with the others, to report back on her findings. And then she told herself that she could simply send them a message over the Link; that there wasn't any need for her to *physically* go and see them.

However, as she was in the process of sending off a message to the others, an idea struck her. She curtailed her path for the room where the wedding dress had been put on display.

Instead, she headed for the lift, and punched the button which would lead her up to the floor on which her office was located.

Once in her office, it was simple to look across the floor and see through the transparent walls. Just as she had suspected, Louise was sat behind Mackenzie's desk, head in hands, sobbing away.

Mackenzie drew in a deep breath.

This was one of her weak points.

Although she had numerous coping strategies—tactics she used to cope with *criers*—these tended to be short-term solutions. Since Mackenzie was most accustomed to such breakdowns accompanying a looming deadline or else a make-or-break meeting, she didn't have much training in seeing things through. In actually *fixing* the problem.

But, then again, who said that there was a problem which *needed* fixing?

Mackenzie shifted along the familiar route, the one which led to her office.

She stepped in through the doorway.

And then waited.

Louise continued to sob away to herself, apparently not having noticed that Mackenzie had even arrived in her office. Finally, though, when she caught something of a hold on herself, she turned her attention upward. Attempted a smile through the tears. And failed.

Deciding that now was the time for her to step in, Mackenzie rounded the desk, arriving behind Louise. She laid a hand down on her shoulder. Gave it a squeeze. She was rewarded by a quivering series of sobs. Mackenzie rounded the chair and then crouched down on her haunches. Out of nowhere, a smile tweaked her lips. "Is it the wrong colour?"

Louise sucked in staccato breaths. Each one seemed to inflate her fractionally more than the previous one. And then she sniffed each one of the laughs back out again. She turned her attention upward, to Mackenzie. This time the smile stuck. As she got herself back under control, taking yet more breaths of air, Louise managed to compose herself sufficiently to get out some words.

"I . . . don't . . . don't . . . *think* . . ."

Sensing that there was someone else present with them, Mackenzie turned around.

She looked off at the corridor.

Realised that Charlie was standing there, in the near darkness.

Although Mackenzie couldn't blame her for having followed—

she had only been concerned for Louise's welfare—it felt as if she had punctured what should've been a private moment between the two of them. Mackenzie reprimanded Charlie in a sharp voice, sending her careening back into the lift, and away from them.

Already feeling regretful that she'd been short with her tone, Mackenzie turned her attention back to Louise. It seemed that Mackenzie's reprimand of Charlie had at least served in allowing Louise a little more recovery time. Some much needed moments to form *words*.

"I don't . . . I *can't* do this."

Not knowing how to respond to this exactly, Mackenzie nodded along, as if she understood the sentiment. She glanced up at Louise. "I'd like to say that I have personal experience— that I know what I'm talking about when it comes to weddings, but I really don't . . . at least when it comes to being on centre stage."

Louise glanced at Mackenzie, looked her in the eye.

Her gaze was profound, as if she was garnering some hidden truth from this comment.

Just what that hidden truth might be—and how it might help Louise in some way—Mackenzie really had no idea.

Finally, Louise averted her gaze, shaking her head. "No," she said. "I don't mean the wedding—I mean . . . I mean . . . *afterwards* . . . I mean that I can't do what comes *afterwards*."

"Oh, you mean the whole getting-lost-in-space thing?"

Louise sniffed a laugh, then looked Mackenzie back in the eye. Her lips slowly moved away from the uneasy smile she'd somehow managed to strike, transforming instead into a stony expression. "What do *you* think?" Louise asked. "What're *you* going to tell Gofreddo?" She gave a shake of her head and then looked out through the window—to the plains beyond. "Forever is a long

time, you know?" She glanced back. "Don't you have any friends—
any *family*—back on Earth?"

Mackenzie thought for a moment. She drew a breath, feeling
her whole body shake as she did so. "I don't suppose there's anyone
in the world who's *really* alone." For the first time, she *really*
thought about what this journey would mean. "There would be
people I'd miss, other people who I'd never get to meet; places
where I'd never get to *go.*" She shrugged. "But, then again, this
could well be the biggest adventure of them all."

Louise looked long and hard at Mackenzie, and then, with a
glimmer in her eye, she gave her a far more solid punch on the arm
than her current state seemed to imply she was capable of . . . it
actually stung quite a bit.

Smiling now, Louise said, "Whoever would've thought that the
mighty dragon Mackenzie Angliss had a corny side?"

And, with that, Louise threw her arms about her.

As Mackenzie endured Louise's embrace, she looked over her
shoulder, out to the lunar plains.

And beyond.

13

EARLY-MORNING ALERT

ackenzie stirred from her sleep with a sudden lurch. She reached up and massaged her poor, aching temples. Then she realised that she had a message awaiting her on the Link. She jabbed her finger into her inner ear.

The message was from Charlie, in Entry Clearance.

All it said was: *White Queen.*

Mackenzie instantly shucked her blankets, making for the overalls which she'd draped over the back of a chair across the room. She quickly zipped herself up, caught a PEAR and arrived to Entry Clearance in what she believed to be record time.

Charlie was waiting for her in the doorway. She looked startled and Mackenzie couldn't help but wonder if she'd only heard the news herself a short while ago. It seemed that she hadn't yet had a chance to interpret and properly react to the development.

'White Queen' was code for Karolin Köhler—*Frau Köhler's*—arrival on the Moon.

To be quite honest, Mackenzie could have done without the surprise visit.

No matter how easily they might communicate with one another—no matter how well they seemed to *get on*—at the end of the day Frau Köhler was her boss.

And it put her on edge to think that she might turn up at any moment of her choosing . . . without previously announcing her arrival.

Then again, there was also the argument which went along the lines that Frau Köhler had absolutely no reason to advise *anyone* of her impending arrival; the Celestial Stays Dome was her own property, after all.

As she paced alongside Charlie, Mackenzie did her best to catch a glimpse of her reflection in a nearby window, looking out onto the lunar plains.

Her appearance was predictably *awful* . . . but she supposed that she didn't have much right to expect anything by way of a miracle. She *had* just rolled out of bed.

It wasn't a difficult task to spot Frau Köhler, she wore the same augmented white hair, jagging down the sides of her face. And if it hadn't been for her appearance alone then it would've been suffi-cient to recognise her by the quantity of well-meaning Celestial Stays employees already buzzing about in her wake. They all seemed keen to do something—carry her *bags*, maybe—but, as always seemed to be the case, Frau Köhler had packed light.

When Frau Köhler's eyes crossed Mackenzie's, she gave her a warm smile.

Mackenzie's heart leaped up into her throat.

She had no idea how Frau Köhler managed to do it; how she could turn out such an *immaculate* appearance on a consistent basis. She had never seen Frau Köhler so much as making small-talk with a makeup artist or a fashion consultant. She always seemed to be alone, tending to herself.

Perhaps there was a shade of truth to some of the unkinder portraits painted of Frau Köhler, that she had something of a 'space witch' about her.

As she always did, Frau Köhler planted a kiss on either of her cheeks by way of greeting before slipping her arm through Mackenzie's, allowing her to lead the way out of Entry Clearance.

"You really *didn't* have to get yourself up to meet me," Frau Köhler said.

Mackenzie felt herself blush. "Really," she replied. "It was no trouble—I always like to be nearby, in case you need anything."

Mackenzie half expected Frau Köhler to throw away this expectation—as she nearly always did . . . this time, though, she didn't. "Well," she said, "it's always a pleasure to see *you*."

Although Mackenzie said nothing to her, Charlie decided to accompany them out to the PEAR and then to the Stellar Tide Cultural Centre—the location which Frau Köhler was keenest to pay a visit to first. Thankfully Mackenzie had the opportunity to alert Julius Denisov—the Guardian in charge of the Stellar Tide—and he greeted them, albeit, like Mackenzie, in a crumpled set of overalls and with a pair of dark bags beneath his eyes.

Mackenzie couldn't help but wickedly wonder if Kyra had been keeping him up late . . .

With Julius taking the lead, Mackenzie had to admit that she was fairly impressed at how coherent he sounded, even though he had got himself up in the middle of the night.

As Mackenzie fell into step alongside Charlie, the two of them following on Julius and Frau Köhler's heels, she was barely conscious of the conversation passing between the two of them— as Julius explained the various cinemas and art galleries and other developments which had replaced the casino which had been there before.

Mackenzie had to admit that she, too, was impressed at the transformation.

When Julius decided to take Frau Köhler into a temporary exposition showcasing lunar photography down the years, Mackenzie hung back in the corridor with Charlie.

It was just after Mackenzie had finished off performing some admin task—firing off a decision in response to an inquiry about tablecloths for Louise and Njhay's wedding—when she couldn't help but turn her attention onto Charlie.

She absorbed the girl—ten years younger, and on her first rotation.

In some ways, Mackenzie had come to see her as a sort of younger sister she'd never had. When Charlie had first been assigned to Mackenzie she recalled how she had seemed callow, and more than a touch doe-eyed. Mackenzie had soon put paid to *those* qualities, though, or so she hoped.

She had given her more than one pep talk on all the usual issues . . . the ones about 'standing up for herself' or else 'speaking up' when she had something to say.

Maybe it was the fact that Mackenzie had been woken up in the middle of her sleep cycle—that she was still feeling dreamy, and not properly filtering her emotions—but she couldn't help but feel a little soppy. Almost like a proud *parent* when she looked over Charlie.

And then she recalled the incident a day before.

When she had reprimanded Charlie, sent her scuttling off

while she had been doing her best to console Louise. "I . . . want to apologise," Mackenzie said. "You know, for *telling you off* when you followed me. You were just doing your job. You wanted to see if there was something you might be able to do to help out. I was wrong to get cross—to send you that fierce look."

At first Charlie blushed deeply, and averted Mackenzie's gaze.

She understood—instinctively, as a matter of fact—that she intimidated the majority of those who dwelled beneath the Celestial Stays Dome; that was the reason why she tried to steer clear of guests as far as possible. But it seemed an especially pertinent observation when she applied it to her relationship with her own personal assistant. Surely if there was one person who should be *unafraid* in her presence, it should be her personal assistant!

Finally, Charlie turned back to Mackenzie—still blushing—but pressing on a smile. It took Mackenzie off guard when she said, "I spent almost the whole of last night crying—I couldn't sleep. I . . . thought that I'd done something very wrong. I thought that I might have . . . uh . . . seen something that I *shouldn't* have seen."

Mackenzie was perplexed by this final comment.

She furrowed her brow.

"What do you mean?"

Charlie tilted her head to one side, looking away from them, to the gallery in which Julius was still giving Frau Köhler a guided tour of the framed photographs—all of them black-and-white prints. "Well, it was that inflight computer—the one which arrived for Gofreddo Zito. And then the rumours. *Everybody* is talking about the mission. About whether or not there is any substance to the gossip." She blinked several times. "I thought you might think that I was *spying* on you; that I was trying to overhear something you might speak with Louise about." She blushed stronger still and when she looked up at her, Mackenzie saw that there were tears glittering in her eyes. "I thought that you might decide to dismiss me. That I had taken a step too . . . *far* . . . that I had been too . . . *presumptive*."

Mackenzie wanted to laugh the matter out of hand.

How could Charlie possibly *believe* that she might be held personally accountable for the rumours which flew about beneath the Celestial Stays Dome?

But, then again, Mackenzie supposed that she had been young once, too.

She had felt as if the world wished her only harm.

Deciding there was only one thing she could do to rectify the situation, she said, "Come here," and reached her arms about Charlie's shoulders, bringing her tightly into her chest; giving her a strong cuddle.

They remained like that until Julius and Frau Köhler finished with their inspection of the photographic gallery. When they returned, Mackenzie and Charlie wore wide smiles.

"Anyone up for some breakfast?" Mackenzie asked.

14

NOSTALGIC MESSAGING

ackenzie was on her way to another meeting addressing Louise and Njhay's wedding when she got a message through from Earthside.

Communication between Celestial Stays employees and the Earth was severely restricted.

Since it was an expensive exercise to get employees onto the Moon, factors which might impact said employee's desire to return to Earth were tightly controlled. It was believed that receiving notification of some monumental event concerning the employee's life down on Earth might adversely impact the performance of their duties beneath the Dome.

And so—after their eighteen-month rotation on Luna—each employee would receive backlogged messages from the period of their service.

Mackenzie, however, overcame such restrictions by the nature of her seniority.

In actual fact, it was Frau Köhler's belief that Mackenzie being restricted from receiving personal Earthside communications might actually restrict her from doing her job to the best of her ability.

Mackenzie had already shown herself to be an outstanding manager of people, their emotions—their particular *issues*—and so, rightly or wrongly, it seemed that Frau Köhler had extended her logic to believe that Mackenzie might be a good manager of her personal life.

As Mackenzie absorbed the message on the Link, she couldn't help but second guess Frau Köhler's assumption here.

The message which'd come through to her was from a familiar name, of course:

Diane Drake.

And, as Mackenzie scanned the contents of the message, as she took in the single, simple line of text which'd been transmitted to her, she couldn't help but feel herself being hurtled at top speed back to her childhood; back to that devastating moment of her youth when she could say—*definitively*—that it had ended, once and for all.

The day she had found out about her parents' death.

It had been Diane Drake—her parents' lawyer—who had finally contacted her.

Mackenzie could recall how—concerned about her parents' late arrival—she had made several phone calls. When she had been unable to get through to either one of her parents, she had tried various, semi-distant family members. They had had no clue either.

In the end, though, she had watched on as an unfamiliar, sleek, black car had pulled up in the driveway of their house. She recalled thinking to herself—*consciously*—about how the car resembled something like a hearse. That sombre thought had remained with her for the entirety of her meeting with Diane Drake.

Although Mackenzie could hardly recall anything of the meeting—anything of what Diane Drake had spoken to her about —the upshot was Mackenzie packing her things and leaving the house with her. They had driven silently for about two hours to a leafy suburb on the outskirts of Sydney. Perhaps Diane had told Mackenzie where they were going—that they were headed for Diane's own home—but it had come as a shock in any case when they had pulled up outside the enormous, seven- or eight-bedroom house with the lush green lawn surrounding it.

Mackenzie recalled how she had become fixated on the thick hedges which had stood on the periphery of the property, each one of them apparently carefully manicured by a tender hand.

Mackenzie soon learned, of course, that Diane employed the services of a specialist gardener; a man called Jack, who was half deaf. In time, she had come to see him almost like an uncle.

When they had arrived, Diane had pointedly shown Mackenzie to her room—spacious and located toward the western extremity of the house.

Mackenzie recalled how she had laid her modest suitcase down at her feet and then looked out of the window to the lake. There had been a variety of ducks and geese bobbing about on the surface.

She couldn't quite remember if Diane had spoken with her much when she had first arrived. She seemed to recall that she had been left mostly to her own devices, with the door to the bedroom closed until night rolled in and—with the gentlest of knocks— Diane had informed her that there was some supper waiting if she felt up to coming downstairs.

Throughout the ensuing months, as Mackenzie's inheritance

was thrashed out, with Diane at the helm, she recalled just sitting and reading as the long days passed her by.

Some days she would take to the garden and read in the sunlight.

This was when Mackenzie would share the half-shouted conversations with Jack the Gardener. He would ask her a question and she would bellow a reply to which he would ask an entirely unrelated question based on her answer. The conversations were not only amusing—on both sides—but also she sensed that the two of them savoured the other's company.

When Diane finished work without fail she would come to see Mackenzie wherever she happened to be. She would then dedicate a solid half an hour to asking Mackenzie how she was—how she was *getting on* . . . the answer was almost always the same; that she was getting through the hours, dealing with what had happened, with the fact that she would no longer see her parents ever again.

And Diane would listen patiently, never asking questions, never pushing or prodding . . . never attempting to garner the extra information which—*surely*—would've made her job sorting out Mackenzie's inheritance spider web go far more smoothly.

She had asked Mackenzie into her home out of simple human empathy. It had seemed—to Diane—the Right Thing to Do.

Mackenzie could only hope that if or when a similar opportunity crossed her path that she would make a similarly benevolent decision.

It was Diane who had encouraged her in her plans to put together her own business with her parents' inheritance. She had been the one who had given her the early support—lots of *free* legal advice and *life* advice to get her moving in the right direction. And she had also been the one who had been responsible for

Mackenzie forming such a solid business backbone; in Mackenzie *forging* a no-nonsense attitude to her business and to her life.

If Mackenzie wished to be taken seriously—and she certainly did—then it was all to do with how she projected herself to the world.

And, by any objective measure, Mackenzie had certainly been taken seriously.

If nothing else.

It was surreal to feel this reminder of her past floating through her brain as she travelled in the PEAR to the latest meeting taking place in the Lunar Grand. Almost as if Diane herself was standing behind her, peeping over her shoulder. She turned over the single line of text in her mind, trying it out from different angles:

You still have so much to give—here on Earth.

15

RETROACTIVE REFLECTIONS

arolin Köhler peered out of the window of the Blue Moon Suite—the room which she had chosen for the duration of her stay beneath the Celestial Stays Dome. On her way here, she had secretly hoped that it might be vacant. Although there would have been no problem in turning out any guests who might have been staying here—she *was* the owner of Celestial Stays, after all—she never would have done something so ... *primadonnaish.*

Despite all of the wealth she had accumulated in the course of her years as CEO of Celestial Stays, she had never fallen into the trap of believing herself as anything other than just another human being among billions. Sure, she had a few more pennies and trinkets than most, but that did nothing to change the fact of who she was.

The Link informed her that there was someone at the door.

Soon after, it informed her that the 'someone' was none other than Gofreddo Zito.

She of course invited him in.

Gofreddo entered with a beaming smile. His eyes—so much like his father's!—twinkled like a pair of precious diamonds . . . or should that have been like a pair of distant stars?

They greeted one another and Karolin instantly felt at ease in his company, as if she was welcoming some long-lost friend.

Although Gofreddo hadn't been responsible for growing a lucrative, international business himself, he had certainly been very much involved with his father as he had done so. He knew about the day-to-day concerns; about how the perception of security which such an apparently 'successful' business breeds with the general public was just that . . . a *perception*.

If only ordinary people realised just how precariously balanced any given business was . . . especially a *successful* one. Goodness knew, Karolin had done her very best to *prevent* Celestial Stays from ever becoming a viable business. She was still doing her best to this very day.

She had done away with the Stellar Tide Casino, giving it a more 'substantial' purpose as a cultural centre. And now she was about to allow her lunar base to play host to the launch of what might well turn out to be the greatest space voyage of their age. Of *any* age.

She gestured to one of the armchairs and Gofreddo took a seat while Karolin remained standing, her hands clasped tightly behind her back. She didn't have long left; and she wasn't about to spend what little remained *sitting down*.

"How are the preparations going?" she asked, in Gofreddo's native Spanish.

"Fine, fine," Gofreddo replied, smiling widely.

"You have everything you need?"

He spread his hands as wide as his smile. "But, of course—thanks to your kind efforts."

Karolin gave a curt nod. Then she peered out through the window, to the lunar plains. She pressed her tongue into the back of her bottom lip, trying to find the words for what she had to say next. It wasn't anything to do with speaking a secondary language—Karolin had taken to studying languages since she was a child—but it was so *difficult* sometimes . . . to say things out loud.

To take that which only existed within her mind's eye and project it out into the wider world.

"And . . . my proposal suits you?" she asked.

At this, Gofreddo's smile faltered slightly. He met Karolin's eye for only a moment, and then he looked out through the glass, to the lunar plains. It was such a common tic when one was up on the Moon—Karolin had noted it with her employees . . . with those who worked for Celestial Stays.

If ever someone felt overwhelmed by the world—if problems seemed insurmountable—they were only to look out through the window, to the lunar plains beyond, and wonder on just how *unlikely* this all was . . . that they were *here*—on the *Moon*.

Finally, Gofreddo replied. "I . . . have no issue," he said. "It would be the least I could do for you—after all you have already given us."

Karolin knew that he was referencing her efforts in helping to have Gofreddo's grandmother buried at the Lunar One Monument; committed to the lunar dust alongside her husband who had perished in the tragedy.

Gofreddo eyed her closely now. He perched on the edge of his armchair. "But are you sure that this is what you want? Can you be *certain* this is what you want?"

Karolin gave him a slight smile by way of reply. "I think it's *always* what I wanted—I have cherished the idea of being an explorer myself; of losing myself in the blackness of space. Of leaving Earth behind forever." She paused. "There's a certain romance in that, don't you think?"

Gofreddo said nothing for a long while.

And then he regained his easy smile.

"I think we are just a pair of old romantics—lost in space and time."

Karolin smiled back. "Yes," she said. "I do too."

16

CONJUGAL ARRANGEMENTS

o say that Mackenzie was losing her mind with three days to go to Njhay and Louise's wedding lacked the drama of the absolute chaos which sprung forth from seemingly every possible location.

It was a wonder that Mackenzie managed to get any sleep at all, although, when she did, it was only to dream that she was present at the ceremony and that all manner of minor tragedies were taking place all around her.

The organist was playing the wrong notes, and out of time.

The guests were in disarray . . . unable to find their places.

And, to top it all off, there was no sign of the bride.

Each and every time, Mackenzie would wake in a cold sweat—heart hammering in her throat. And she could never quite manage to calm herself down. She had to reassure herself that she still had time—that there was *still* time for everything to be put *right* . . . and yet, she couldn't help but feel that everything had already spun clean out of control. And that she was being childish to bury her head in the sand and pretend that everything was okay.

The first step to solving a problem was acknowledging that it even existed.

Then there was that lingering doubt about the message which Diane Drake had sent to her:

You still have so much to give—here on Earth.

Mackenzie had taken the opportunity to send off what she planned to do to a few choice people she trusted down on Earth. She had received measured replies from all of them, although every response had—almost uniformly, albeit in myriad ways— told her that she should do 'whatever she *felt* was right'. The only one who had come down on any sort of side of the issue was Diane.

But did the simple fact that she was a dissenting voice among an enthusiastic crowd mean that she could be disregarded?

Mackenzie was unsure.

She wondered what the message's exact intent was.

Did Diane just wish for Mackenzie to think long and hard about this decision?

. . . No, surely Diane knew her well enough to know she would make the right decision in the end. Then, if Diane was not attempting to swing Mackenzie one way or another, perhaps she was just trying to remind Mackenzie of something which she had forgotten—something which she had left behind in the past. To tell the truth, Mackenzie didn't believe that there was anything else left for her down on Earth. She couldn't help but feel that she had no *reason* to return.

Of course, she would love to see Diane—for the two of them to 'catch up'.

But then what?

Mackenzie could, of course, begin again with another business —once she had got done with her Celestial Stays service. She could build something else from the ground up. She supposed—for a time—she would find pleasure from that.

But once she'd brought it to fruition what would she do?

The very prospect of this—akin to looking into an impenetrable void—was near paralysing for her. So much so that she nearly neglected to notice the message which had just arrived to her inbox. It was from Louise. Asking her where she'd got to.

With a quick glance in the mirror—and a *quicker* smudge of makeup about the eyes—Mackenzie headed out of her apartment, catching the PEAR to the Lunar Grand.

It seemed Mackenzie had arrived just on time.

When she turned up to the meeting, she was taken slightly off guard to find that Frau Köhler was there. She just about managed to catch herself—to fire a smile off in her direction—before the realisation completely left her high and dry.

Charlie was awaiting her just inside the room, too, of course.

When Mackenzie was on the cusp of giving her a muttered reprimand—for not informing her that Frau Köhler would be present at the meeting—she recalled that she *had* received a message earlier from Charlie, telling her this exact fact.

God, she *really was* getting sloppy.

Next thing she knew, she'd be forgetting to put on her overalls before leaving her apartment. Wasn't that how these things progressed? One little slip-up at a time . . .

She looked about the others present—Alicia, Kyra, Lan and *Louise.*

All of the girls.

All of those who would be travelling on Gofreddo's ship . . . Frau Köhler and Charlie excepted.

Mackenzie turned her attention to the hologram of the Celestial Stays Dome which was set before them. She had ordered the holographic model constructed so that they could better visualise the wedding ceremony itself. As had already been agreed, the ceremony would take place in the Crescent Gardens. And—as Mackenzie had envisaged—the static hologram already featured an assortment of marquees; guests and waiters dotted about among the canvases. There was even a rendering of Njhay and Louise there—dressed up in their bride-and-groom attire.

"Ready?" Alicia asked, arching an eyebrow at Mackenzie.

Mackenzie knew that this was a subtle jibe at her for being the last to arrive when she was—almost without exception—the first on the scene. It was only the way in which Mackenzie would react if someone had had the nerve to arrive late to some meeting she had plotted out herself. Mackenzie gave a nod.

And Alicia activated the model.

The lights in the room dimmed.

And the hologram before them became almost *brilliantly* bright in the darkness.

Its static image faded, replaced by a moving representation.

There was no sign of the bride and groom standing together now—only the Crescent Gardens decked out and seemingly awaiting the ceremony about to take place.

Mackenzie paid attention to the details—to the PEARs, now coloured a matrimonial silver-white; to the way in which the plants themselves seemed to have taken on a ghostly hue; how there was the dim sound of a string quartet playing in the background.

Slowly, the figures began to move.

Almost unconsciously, Mackenzie took a step closer to the hologram.

She stooped over to get a better look.

She located Njhay. He looked fetching in his wedding suit, with Gofreddo Zito—who else?!—as his best man, standing nobly at his side.

Gradually, the seats which were laid out before the altar—formed out of greenery—were filled by the arriving guests.

Mackenzie was struck by the attention to detail, able to make out not just herself and the girls present here, but also the faces of the other employees of Celestial Stays.

She supposed that whoever had put together the hologram had accessed some sort of a database and drawn the physical manifestations from it.

As Mackenzie observed the ceremony sped up to about fifty or a hundred times, the day lights in the Dome gradually gave way to night. Measured, silver and gold lights glimmered about in the foliage surrounding the marquees; the seats were removed; and a dance floor emerged out of seemingly nothing at all.

Despite herself, Mackenzie felt a few tears welling in the corners of her eyes.

Thankfully, though, once the demonstration had ended and the lights had been turned back up to their former intensity, she had managed to get herself back under control.

However, she wasn't able to control the smile which snuck onto her lips.

"Well," she said, aware that everyone in the room was staring at her—waiting with bated breath for her reaction to the plan as it had unfurled. "This will certainly be a wedding to be remembered

—I'll have to thank whoever put this hologram together person-ally. It really captures the imagination, doesn't it?"

When Mackenzie glanced up, she realised that Alicia and Louise were staring back at her with smirks smeared all over their faces.

Finally, Alicia spoke, "You can thank him right now if you feel like it."

Confused, she turned around, to the doorway, and saw who was standing there.

Miguel Cruz.

17

CONFLICT OF LOGIC

iguel had entered the scene about thirty seconds after the hologram had begun to play.

He had watched on as his rendering of Njhay and Louise's wedding had come to life between the women. Although he had most enjoyed Mackenzie's reaction, he had been especially keen to see how Karolin Köhler might react.

Throughout she had paid close attention—a smile lining her lips the entire time.

It hadn't been a difficult task for him to put together the model. In fact, he couldn't claim to have *created* the model at all; he had merely searched for the appropriate files within the Armstrong Archive and then worked on adding the animations. There had been a time when he had thought long and hard about entering the world of computer-modelling before eventually deciding that his true passion lay in the preservation and organisation of knowledge; what he saw to be a higher-level calling.

All of the women were looking at him, and Miguel couldn't

help but blush. He had never been all that terrific when it came to social occasions—when it came to working in a *team* . . . he had always thought that he fared best when he was alone with his thoughts.

When he could dedicate time to his own mind and the many —*many*—materials which lay in the Archive for him to discover.

Finally, though, once the women had got through with congratulating him, he found his attention lingering on Louise Williams. He saw how she had gone quite pale. How she had bowed her head slightly, still taking in the holographic model in its static form.

She looked up.

Smiled faintly.

"It's perfect," she said. "Just how I imagined it."

Miguel felt a warm glow pass through his bloodstream.

He smiled back at her.

"I am very glad," he replied.

As the meeting reached its apparent end, and the women began to file out, he noticed that Mackenzie stayed behind. He was so distracted that he almost didn't notice Frau Köhler laying her hand on his shoulder and giving it a squeeze, offering him her own hearty congratulations. It was all he could do to mutter something about it being a very simple thing to cobble together.

But it didn't seem to mitigate her enthusiasm any.

Once Miguel was alone with Mackenzie, it was inevitable that the doubt which had crept into his mind would rise to the surface. Even as he looked her over—as he looked her *gorgeous* body over— he couldn't help but know exactly what he had to say.

He waited until the footsteps of the others had faded from the room, and Mackenzie's personal assistant—Charlie—had made herself scarce.

His and Mackenzie's eyes met for the longest time, and he knew that both of them were thinking about *that* kiss. He thought about how she had surprised him; how he had simply had no time to react. He felt as if he had been a *passenger* to that kiss.

The *object*.

It had been some sort of test which Mackenzie had administered him.

And only one question remained.

Had he passed or failed?

Mackenzie took a few steps toward him, a slight smile hanging off the corner of her mouth. She arched an eyebrow. "That really was an impressive display," she said.

She came closer still.

Close enough so that he could feel her body heat.

He was surprised that he managed to keep his voice firm —*unwavering*.

"I really can't take any of the credit—it was just something which I whipped up from the Archive."

"All the faces," she said, still smiling, "they were of the Celestial Stays employees; the ones who will actually attend the ceremony. How did you come up with that? How did you manage to *do* that?"

He shrugged. "It was the simplest solution," he said. "We keep on record physical representations of all our employees. They were at hand. *Convenient*."

She moved closer still.

He breathed the subtle scent of strawberries.

Her perfume?

"Well," Mackenzie continued, holding her ground now. "I was *very* impressed."

It was difficult to tell if this was or wasn't another test.

He wondered if she might want to see whether or not he was attracted to her.

Whether or not he was *really* attracted to her.

If that was the case then it would've been far more efficient for her to simply ask the question . . . because he was certain of his reply.

He pushed these concerns away for the time being. He was going to have to confide his doubts about the mission in someone and it seemed that it might as well be Mackenzie Angliss as anyone else. Just so that they knew where they stood.

He turned to her, settling into a new sense of determination "I . . . don't think I'm going to accept the place on the ship."

He watched on as Mackenzie went through the range of emotions in reacting to this claim.

First there were the pert lips, as if she was calculating just what he was *trying* to say, and then there were the fine worry lines which appeared in her brow.

Finally there was the cocked head and look of out-and-out concern.

As if Miguel had lost his mind.

"Why?" she asked.

A tightness settled in across Miguel's chest.

He had prepared his answer, of course.

He *always* knew what he had to say.

"I've been doing the reading," he said, unable to look her in the eye now—he felt almost like a doctor delivering bad news about a patient to a close family member. "And it seems to me that this . . . this *plan* of Gofreddo's is not much beyond a vanity project." This time he summoned the courage to look her in the eye. "All of the experts—throughout history—they are united in their consensus."

"And what's their 'consensus'?"

The way that Mackenzie intoned the word—'consensus'—sent a shudder running down Miguel's spine. It was almost as if he was throwing around some controversial theory; almost as if *he* was the one in the wrong!

"They all agree that it would be far more efficient—not to mention more *practical*—to send probes out into space. To have unmanned machines do the exploring for us."

Miguel wondered if he should add anything else.

But he decided that—as usual—he had summed things up fairly succinctly.

He waited for Mackenzie's response.

Finally, she glanced up at him.

Met his eye.

"To be quite honest," she said, "I'm having doubts myself . . ."

Miguel felt a strange rising sensation through his body, as if he had suddenly lost ten kilos. He looked deeply into Mackenzie's green eyes, as if he might be able to read the thoughts which were currently funnelling through her brain.

But—as with all women—she was an enigma to him.

He decided to break the uneasy silence between them.

"And what do you think we should do about it?" he said.

Mackenzie was silent for a long while—apparently stewing in her thoughts; trying to come to some conclusion. Then she looked back at him.

Miguel felt his stomach sink.

"I think that we should sit on it—each one should make the decision for themselves. This isn't something that we should just decide on a *whim*."

Miguel couldn't help wondering if Mackenzie wasn't truly a woman after his own heart.

18

CONTINUITY PLANNING

$\mathcal{M}$ackenzie *glanced up from her desk,* seeing that Charlie was standing at the door to her office. She realised now that there was no other option. That she had to call her in for the chat.

She could only put this off—put the *future* off—for so long.

Charlie smiled nervously before sitting in the chair opposite.

She fidgeted several times before finding any sort of comfort.

Mackenzie realised just what Charlie must've been feeling— that she was no doubt anxious to find out for what reason she had been called to her office. And Mackenzie would soon dispel her concerns. In a matter of moments, even.

"You remind me a lot of myself," Mackenzie said, and then grimaced openly at how she had somehow allowed *that* cliché to sneak free of her lips.

Charlie, though, seemed unabashed.

Keen for Mackenzie to say more.

"What have you thought of your time up here—beneath the Dome—so far?"

Although Mackenzie was certain this would not be an easy question to answer in the presence of a superior, she was also fairly certain that if anyone had the requisite *nerve* to give an honest response then it would be Charlie. And, if she didn't, then Mackenzie would just have to admit that she had proven herself wrong.

Charlie gazed out of the window, to the lunar plains, for several moments.

Mackenzie was very aware of these times.

When someone took the opportunity to think things over Very Carefully on the Moon they often used the lunar plains to aid their thought processes; to find whatever plane of their consciousness they required to root out the answer.

Finally, Charlie replied to her.

"I have learned a lot," she said. "And in a very short time. Before I arrived here—to the Moon—I did not have all that much experience working with guests, working with *clients* . . . it has been a sharp learning curve for me, but I believe that I have slowly put the pieces together. That I have *slowly* started to understand how the mechanisms work."

Mackenzie was satisfied enough with the surface-level answer.

But, in truth she had expected something more.

Just *a little more* so that she could be one-hundred-per-cent certain of her gut instinct.

However, there was no need for Mackenzie to prompt Charlie. She seemed to sense what was required of her.

"Some parts of the experience are uncomfortable," Charlie said. "I miss my family—living in communal facilities has been more difficult than I imagined it would be." She smiled wryly. "Lots of *unanticipated* problems . . . a lot of issues which I did not believe would be issues." She glanced out of the window again briefly, then continued, "I think life on the Moon shall be extremely difficult for me. A real *challenge*."

It was now that Mackenzie noticed a few tears had appeared on the surface of Charlie's eyes—to begin with it gave her the air of a doll . . . something that wasn't *quite* real.

Charlie suddenly reached across the table, snatching hold of Mackenzie's wrists.

She squeezed tightly—so tightly that her grip cut off Mackenzie's circulation.

Mackenzie had the sudden thought of calling for help.

As if—*somehow*—she might be in danger.

Finally, though, she got a hold of herself.

Told herself that this was Charlie; her trusted personal assistant she was afraid of.

She caught a hold on her anxiety.

And saw the fear just beneath the surface of Charlie's eyes.

This was Mackenzie's time to be patient.

She had asked the question which would elicit this response.

Now it was her charge to deal with the consequences.

And so Mackenzie exercised her patience.

She waited for Charlie to calm down.

And slowly—*surely*—Charlie eased her grip on Mackenzie's wrists.

As Charlie sank back into her chair, taking deep breaths as she got herself back under control, Mackenzie wondered at her own negligence—at allowing Charlie to go so long when she had such *obvious* issues surrounding her time beneath the Dome.

"As I was saying," Mackenzie continued, with a calm voice. "You remind me so much of myself—of when I was driven to succeed. Of when I did things which scared me. Of when I suffered through challenging situations so that I might have grown professionally and personally."

When Mackenzie looked over Charlie, she realised she was absorbing each and every one of her words. She was listening to her with intense care.

Hearing her out.

Mackenzie knew that Charlie wouldn't believe her—wouldn't *really* believe her—until much later. Perhaps *years* later. And yet she knew that she had to have this chat now; that it would've been negligent of her to *not* take the opportunity to speak with her about her future.

Once Mackenzie was convinced that Charlie had recovered from her outpouring, she sent her on her way, watching her head into the lift; the doors sliding shut behind her.

Convinced that Charlie was really gone, Mackenzie dialled into the Link and began to compose a message to Frau Köhler. She had decided that—once she was certain—there would be no reason for her to delay recommending her replacement; whether that replacement would be instantaneous, or several years hence, it was Mackenzie's responsibility to let Frau Köhler know.

Because, Mackenzie was decided, if she did not take her place on Gofreddo's crew then she would return to Earth. It felt as if she had slipped into life on the Moon easily.

Perhaps a little *too* easily.

Now was the time for a fresh challenge.

A new start.

And she had nobody but Diane Drake to thank for the reminder.

19

SPECIAL-EVENT SCHEMATICS

*S*trangely, Mackenzie managed to sleep through the entire night before the wedding.

She supposed that she had had so much time to stew over every last detail in the previous weeks that she—quite simply—no longer had the mental reserves to deal herself any more nightmare scenarios. She had made herself suffer for long enough.

Now was the time for her to just go through the motions of all that she had set in place.

But that was more easily said than done.

Mackenzie had hardly got up onto her feet—let alone jumped in the shower and got dressed—before she felt a barrage of messages arriving on the Link; all of them seemingly *urgently* seeking her. Thinking quickly, she delegated to Charlie that which didn't catch her eye at first pass; or that which was obviously the domain of another Division.

In the end, she had given herself three options to choose from for Louise and Njhay's wedding.

She had laid them out on their hangers so that she might be able to pick which one would best serve her needs on the day itself.

The first option was a sensible, no-nonsense, trouser suit.

It was the royal-blue of Celestial Stays.

Without so much as a second glance, Mackenzie moved to the next option.

The second option was a *smouldering* black cocktail dress.

Although the dress itself was a fine design—one of Alicia's better efforts—Mackenzie couldn't help but think that black just didn't go all that well with a wedding.

There was too much of an air of a *funeral* to it.

Finally, realising that she was rapidly narrowing the range of her options, Mackenzie found herself looking over her last potential outfit.

It was a fun yellow dress the hem of which floated down about the heels.

Mackenzie had thought of this dress as being something like her 'soul dress'.

It seemed . . . dare she say it? . . . *adventurous.*

Even when she brought the dress down over her head, she felt herself beginning to tingle all over.

Her heart thrummed in her ribcage.

When she looked herself over in the mirror, she had to admit that she was somewhat taken aback by the stark contrast of the yellow material with her *shockingly* red hair.

There would be no missing her at the ceremony.

Mackenzie had never been a person to flip-flop.

Of course, she didn't like to *leap* into decisions without fully considering the implications, but, on the other hand, when she did settle on a decision her mind was certain to remain made up. This had been another of Diane Drake's pep talks; about how she shouldn't *openly* show indecisiveness while still maintaining an open mind to new information.

She should always be ready to be proven wrong, but, at the same time, once she'd settled on a path it was better to keep on walking it until it became obvious that she'd taken a wrong turn.

Now fully dressed, Mackenzie caught a PEAR to the Crescent Gardens.

As she went on her way, she delegated the last of the remaining tasks on the Link then switched to Standby so that she might have a moment's rest—a few *quiet* moments—to take in just how the arrangements for the wedding were shaping up.

When she stepped over the side of the PEAR, she was prepared for just about anything. She was prepared for a whole host of employees to come running up to her, each and every one of them with some sort of a horror story to spill.

But things seemed quiet.

Strangely quiet.

She drew a profound breath, felt the air tingle about her lungs, and then she trod her way in through the entrance of the Gardens.

Another lesson she had picked up from Diane Drake was the *Art* of Management.

Lots of people seemed to believe that good management could be defined by how 'hands on' any given boss happened to be. However, Diane had on several occasions warned Mackenzie away from doing things which were 'outside her skillset'.

Mackenzie was here to keep things organised, and she could hardly do that effectively or efficiently if she was erecting an altar, while baking the wedding cake as she set about arranging the cards with the seating places marked.

Even years on, though, it was a difficult lesson for her to absorb.

She still felt the familiar urge to *help out.*

Before long, Mackenzie observed the procession of 'helpers' arriving to the Gardens.

She watched on as Alicia Brennan—along with a team of kitchen staff sourced from the Lunar Grand—shepherded along a whole swarm of drones; each one of them containing some item of food. When an especially large drone whined past, Mackenzie decided that this drone's specific task had to be transporting the wedding cake.

That was *another* thing off her mind.

Mackenzie thought about that other piece of advice which Diane Drake had offered her—that once Mackenzie *did* learn to let go, when she came to see that she simply *couldn't,* micromanage every last thing, she would feel a strange sense of freedom dawning over her.

Sort of like the sensation of all the pieces of a puzzle falling into place as she just stood by and watched on.

And that was how Mackenzie was beginning to feel right now.

A few minutes later, Kyra Singh arrived with a squadron of photographers at her heel.

Mackenzie smiled pleasantly at her—and Kyra grinned back.

Kyra was wearing a golden sari typical of her culture.

Mackenzie watched on as Kyra—with the photographers in tow—headed for the spot which had been demarcated for them to populate.

A raised platform slightly to the side of the area which would allow the photographers a perfect vantage point of the audience, and the couple as they arrived at the altar.

She also observed Julius Denisov, who was dashing about seeing to little details.

Mackenzie had enlisted him—and his expertise in putting on events; both legitimate and decidedly *shady*—to bring anything and everything to her attention.

He wore a sober, charcoal suit with a pearl-coloured tie knotted about his throat. He nodded to Mackenzie as he passed by, taking a moment to inspect one of the coverings of the chairs all arranged and directed at the altar.

Soon after, Mackenzie nearly had a heart attack when Lan Niu turned up at her elbow.

Lan wore a blazing-red satin robe with silver and gold designs weaved into the fabric.

To be quite honest, Mackenzie hadn't recognised her until she had subtly indicated the blaster pistol strapped to the inside of her thigh. There would be no security breaches on Lan's watch . . .

As the preparations were in the process of being finalised, Mackenzie allowed herself to fall into the background—something which she supposed more easily said than done what with the combination of red hair and yellow dress.

Soon, the guests began to arrive and Mackenzie lurked nearby while the employees of the Dome helped them find their seats before the altar. There was a whole range of dress on show—something which reflected the variety of cultures present beneath the Celestial Stays Dome. Mackenzie couldn't help wondering to herself if there had ever been such a multicultural wedding in human history . . . perhaps that was a question which she could pose to Miguel Cruz.

"Hi."

It was then that Mackenzie turned.

And found herself locking eyes with none other than Miguel.

All of a sudden, she went all hot over.

And then cold—*impossibly* cold.

She managed to catch herself long enough to absorb his appearance. He had on a well-cut jacket over the top of a tight-fitting pair of trousers. Beneath he wore a fine cloth shirt with a lilac-coloured tie about his neck. Despite herself, Mackenzie couldn't quite get the words out as fluently as she would've liked. "You've . . . scrubbed *up* well."

Miguel gave a slight smile. "Thanks," he replied. "You don't look too bad yourself."

She felt herself blush. She shifted her attention away from Miguel, and to the guests who were assembling in the seats.

"Anything I can do to help?" he asked.

She was shaking her head before she'd even replied. Sensing this, she attempted to mitigate the cold reaction with a slight smile. "No," she said. "I don't think so—just find your seat and get settled in for the ceremony." She attempted to widen her smile, but felt that her effort had more the effect of a snarl than a grin.

If Miguel noted Mackenzie's cool tone then he made no outward showing of it.

He merely gave a nod—*another smile*—and then took his seat among the arriving guests.

Mackenzie stood stunned for several moments before she realised that almost everyone was in place. That all of the guests had *arrived*.

As she scanned the seats toward the front of the audience, she noticed that there were still some empty places. She knew who they belonged to, of course . . . and—

It was then that Mackenzie caught sight of Frau Köhler making her way toward her assigned seat.

Charlie paced along in her wake.

Mackenzie had assigned Charlie to look after Frau Köhler for the duration of today—for the wedding. That had been one of the most difficult tasks of delegation she had had to go through with. To hand over the wellbeing of Frau Köhler to one of her subordinates.

But, then again, Charlie wasn't just *any* subordinate— Mackenzie had chosen her to be her successor.

She needed to trust her judgement.

Her *gut*.

Charlie would do a good job . . . and—in any case—it wasn't like Frau Köhler was an unforgiving boss; she had been *extremely* generous toward Mackenzie in her role as Supervisor of Human Resources so there was no reason to believe she would be any different with Charlie, or whoever ended up getting Mackenzie's past role.

Once everybody had slotted into place, Mackenzie glanced about the whole area, eager to spot any Nascent Issues before they became Insurmountable Problems.

Nothing that leaped out at her.

All the guests in place.

The registrar standing at the altar.

And the string quartet tuning up.

It was then that she cast a final glance over the audience—saw that all of the chairs were occupied. Just as she was about to send the prompt through the Link which would commence the ceremony, she paused. There was something which stopped her sending the order.

When she caught hold of herself, she realised that it was a head turned back from the crowd.

A pair of eyes staring at her.

Miguel Cruz.

The two of them stared at one another for no more than a few seconds, but—to Mackenzie—it felt far more like several *hours*.

Feeling her stomach turning itself into knots, she returned to the present moment.

To the Link.

And to the decision to *begin*.

She gave the order.

It was one of those moments when Mackenzie was sure she would faint.

Although she had never had much in common with renaissance women, she *had* fainted on more than one occasion. Gladly, these occasions had always been when she was on her own. Nobody had ever *seen* her in the act of fainting. And she was determined that now would be no different.

As soon as she began to feel frail, she reached out for a nearby railing and steadied herself. She continued to stand behind the audience, on a raised platform. She enjoyed the view and sense of power which the position granted her.

It made her feel as if she was in more control of that which was about to pass; even though, in reality, she had ceded control to others—she had *delegated* to others.

It began as a non-distinct *hum* in the distance.

Mackenzie remained standing still, turning her thoughts back to the holographic model which Miguel had put together to show how the ceremony would look once it had started.

Even though the model had been a wonderful feat of artistry—no matter how hard Miguel attempted to play it down—there was no comparison to the real thing.

Because, just like the audience, she was seeing it unfold in reality for the first time.

Seeing that the audience had turned their necks in the direction of the sound, Mackenzie did the same. She followed the group gaze.

It was just possible to make out the looming shape as it came closer.

Swiftly, Mackenzie made sense of the object.

A Lunar Shuttle.

She felt rooted to the spot as the Shuttle approached, as it hovered inevitably toward the Gardens.

The *hum* shifted into a menacing *roar* as it passed over their heads.

Mackenzie bent her neck backward and took in the underside of the Shuttle, seeing—for a moment—the tubes and wires and inner-workings of the craft.

The Shuttle continued over the audience, and to the altar, where it hovered.

Just like the others, Mackenzie stood and watched in wonder as a ladder descended from the underside of the Shuttle and a pair of figures began to lower themselves down the rungs. Although it was impossible to make out more than a pair of suits—a pair of *men*—from where Mackenzie stood, she of course knew that this was Njhay and Gofreddo.

Njhay picked his way down carefully to the ground while Gofreddo couldn't resist a spirited, boyish jump from about a metre up. As he bent his knees for the landing, it was possible to make out the smile which seemed to occupy his entire face. He held up his arms in a victory pose and the audience gave a spontaneous round of applause coupled with a few rounds of *whooping*.

When Mackenzie turned her attention onto Njhay, she couldn't help but think that he looked just a *shade* less confident than Gofreddo before this audience.

In fact, he was picking at the buttons on the cuffs of his suit jacket as if there was a loose thread he just couldn't manage to tear free. When he did look up at the audience, apparently reacting to the audience's applause for Gofreddo's feat in jumping down the last rungs of the ladder, he wore a sheepish expression. And Mackenzie was fairly certain that he was *blushing* . . . even looking on from a distance. Then again, who was Mackenzie to judge?

She had never featured in a starring role in a wedding.

She had only ever been an attending guest.

Or, like now, the organiser.

It was with this realisation on her mind that she found herself impulsively looking back to where Miguel was sitting. But this time he didn't look around—he seemed just as captivated by this surprising arrival as the rest of the guests.

As the Shuttle droned on out of view, there was an unsteady— slightly *uncomfortable*—silence which draped across the crowd.

She looked to Gofreddo, wondering if he might make one of his eccentric quips to lighten the mood. But it seemed that even he was aware that this event had nothing to do with him; that this was Njhay and Louise's day.

Mackenzie couldn't help herself snarkily wondering if Gofreddo was only willing to give Njhay and Louise their day on the understanding that all the days in the future would belong to him . . . perhaps there had been something to Miguel's claim that Gofreddo's proposal was merely a 'vanity project'.

Soon enough, Mackenzie sensed the droning of another Shuttle drawing close.

She shifted her attention off to the horizon.

Like before, her mind had trouble distinguishing the object.

But then she brought it clear.

This particular Shuttle—Mackenzie soon saw—had been adorned with a white, silk ribbon which flapped with the motion of the craft.

Even though Mackenzie had always believed that she had a high tolerance when it came to sentiment—that she wasn't likely to break down in tears at just about anything—she couldn't help thinking, as she observed the Shuttle coming closer and closer, that she might be about to lose control.

Indeed—as the Shuttle passed over the audience, everyone craning their neck upward to take in the sight—Mackenzie felt a couple of tears squeeze free of the corners of her eyes.

She reached up and wiped them off her cheeks.

By the time the Shuttle was hovering over the altar—just above Njhay and Gofreddo's heads—Mackenzie hoped there was no trace of her tears.

No trace of her *weakness*.

This time a drone-powered platform descended to the altar.

Louise's wedding dress made her seem factors of sizes larger than she truly was. She looked like an angel . . . or that was what Mackenzie thought.

Patrick Fourie—the Shuttle pilot—stood beside her as they made their way down.

Gradually, the Shuttle—running on autopilot now—hummed

away from the audience and back toward the Hangar as the string quartet started up.

The platform carrying Patrick and Louise descended the final distance to the ground.

To the altar.

Like the gentleman he assuredly was, Patrick stepped off the platform first before offering Louise his hand, to support her stepping down behind him.

With the bride and groom at the altar, Mackenzie felt herself beginning to well up again.

But she swallowed hard and turned her attention to what was to come—and what she might be able to do to control it.

The ceremony—the wedding vows themselves—passed almost in a dream.

Mackenzie supposed it was because she had pictured the scene in her mind so many times.

She had *dreamed* about this sight so many times.

And now it was unfolding before her in reality . . . never to be repeated.

The wedding vows were over almost as soon as they had started. The couple were congratulated by the registrar and the audience applauded as they kissed.

Mackenzie supposed that she might've been the most emphatic in her applause.

Her palms stung once she had got through with the clapping.

She blinked several times—as if clearing her vision of a daze—and then set her mind to that which was to come.

The *celebration*.

Again, it was just as it had played out in Mackenzie's mind—at least in her positive moments.

The employees moved in once the guests had been gestured away from the happy couple and off to a side-lined grove of the Crescent Gardens.

They worked to stack the chairs, to clear space for the dining table.

Mackenzie worked quickly, leaving her place behind and going off to confer with Alicia.

Alicia was nothing but smiles as Mackenzie hung about in her wake, watching as she effortlessly guided her staff about their task—how she gracefully dismissed any problem or concern which was raised with her. She seemed to have an answer for everything.

Mackenzie couldn't help thinking that Alicia would've been the perfect replacement for her if she hadn't set her heart on jetting off into the stars with her boyfriend.

Actually, Alicia would've been an improvement in just about *every* area.

She had already demonstrated herself a natural manager.

An *instinctive* leader of people.

Once the photographs were done with, Mackenzie spoke with Kyra and they conspired to bring the guests back to the now-laid table replete with all manner of delicious food.

The option they had gone for in the end was something of a mix between Filipino and British.

For the starter they had selected asparagus and cheese muffins along with pumpkin soup and barbecued broccoli with goats' cheese. The idea was for the guests to pick and choose from the many dishes which were presented them.

Mackenzie watched on—not with any small hunger—as the

silver trays bearing the starter course were carried out to the waiting guests.

Finally, Alicia flapped and fussed enough so that Mackenzie felt there was no choice for her but to leave the kitchen behind.

Unless she wanted Alicia to decapitate her with one of those handily positioned cleavers . . .

Mackenzie took up her place at the table. As she had arranged it, she was sandwiched between Frau Köhler and Charlie. William Duval—Supervisor of Security—sat opposite her, his doting wife alongside. Then there was Refilwe Mbemba, Supervisor of Tourism, who was already tucking in with great anticipation to one of the asparagus and cheese muffins. Mackenzie hadn't bothered to assign Alicia a seat at the table—despite her being a Supervisor—deciding, correctly it seemed, that she would have her hands full in the kitchen.

It was only a secondary thought—as she indulged in the deliciously seasoned pumpkin soup—that she hoped Alicia would get the chance to savour the food she had so lovingly put together with the aid of her kitchen staff.

Mackenzie felt almost dreary when the starters were finished with.

If she hadn't had her figure to worry about then she might well have indulged in several more portions of all three options. However, it appeared to be a good thing that she had left room for what was coming next.

She recalled the conversation she'd had with Alicia as the kitchen staff brought out the main courses. This was all Philippine Adobo. The various dishes featured chicken and beef and pork; and all of it smothered with vinegar, soy sauce and garlic.

Mackenzie wasn't certain she'd be able to contain herself as she observed the food being brought out on yet more of the silver trays. The smells alone were enough to drive her wild; enough to send jiggling sensations through her gut and a shudder up her spine.

As she tucked into the main course, she felt herself entering something of a dream state, almost as if she could hardly bring herself to quite believe the culinary pleasure taking place within her mouth. She shovelled rice onto her plate, and tried out each one of the options.

By the end, she was fairly certain that she was reaching the point of bursting.

But that was when they brought out the desserts.

This time, it was Louise's culture which was given preference.

It was to be British-influenced choices.

Mackenzie hungrily—*somehow!*—eyed the sticky-toffee pudding and the carrot cake and the blackberry-and-apple crumble. She took in how the kitchen staff offered the option of whipped cream or ice cream to accompany the main dessert.

Once they had finished eating, Mackenzie couldn't help but flinch at the odd sight of the champagne being brought out by the kitchen staff.

Although lunar laws prohibited the consumption of alcohol—or other behaviour-altering substances—she had succeeded in gaining official permission down Earthside.

Of course, it had helped Mackenzie a great deal that Frau Köhler had greased up those involved in the decision-making process.

The speeches and the toasts passed in a blur.

She was only dimly aware of the mechanical scheduling of everything—of everything going *just* as she had planned.

With the champagne swilling about her belly, and the bubbles seeming almost to throb through her bloodstream, she could hardly take her eyes off Njhay and Louise—the two of them looked so *happy*.

Was that the secret?

Finding someone who shared your world view?

Or just someone you could *stand*?

Company?

. . . Was that what was missing from Mackenzie's life?

With this seeming insight jolting through her mind, Mackenzie couldn't help but feel a touch sombre as—with all the other guests —she left the dining table behind; adjourning again to the demarcated area while the staff cleared up for the dancing to come.

She realised she'd never felt so solitary—so *alone*—as when she took her leave from the table; as she merged with the crowd.

EMBARRASSMENT MATRIX

s Miguel took in the crowds as they peeled away from the dining table, it was all that he could do to think of anything but just how *full* he was . . . and how he had—*just perhaps* —overindulged in all the delicious food which'd been lain before him. The champagne had hardly done wonders for his digestion, although he certainly felt the rush of blood flooding up to his brain.

That was *one* benefit of alcohol.

It did get his heart beating just that touch faster.

Miguel mingled with the guests as he supped on what remained of his champagne. He had never been a big drinker and the tolerance for alcohol he had built up from what little drinking he had done down on Earth had now deserted him totally. He felt lightheaded. *Wreckless* even.

As he passed through the faces—some anonymous and others *not* so anonymous—he couldn't help but realise that he was searching for something.

Or *someone* . . .

It didn't take long to realise it was Mackenzie he sought.

He swept the crowds, hoping to catch sight of her flame-red hair, or that delicious yellow dress she had decided to wear for the occasion. It had shocked him when he had first seen her. He was so used to seeing her in the drab, royal-blue Celestial Stays overalls. To begin with, he had believed that she was another woman *entirely*. And then he'd been infinitely glad to realise that it really was Mackenzie. Of course there was still the question which continued to linger on his mind, namely that their future hung on what they planned to do; whether or not they would choose to join Gofreddo's mission to the stars . . . his *Quest* to the Stars as Miguel had heard Kyra refer to the plans in her tabloidlike manner.

It didn't take long to pick Mackenzie out of the crowd.

She *was* somewhat distinctive.

Perhaps on another day—if he hadn't already gorged himself on wonderful food and then swigged a decent portion of champagne—Miguel would've been content to stick to the shadows; to observe from a distance. But it felt that today everything was different. That he *himself* was a different person. And he knew that he had to seize upon the opportunity.

Because it might not ever come again.

He immediately observed that Mackenzie was deep in conversation with someone familiar. It was only when he had drawn much closer—*he wasn't wearing his glasses*—that he realised just who it was:

Frau Karolin Köhler.

He was halfway through the process of backing away from the two of them when Mackenzie caught his eye. He turned his head, as if the gesture itself would make him invisible.

It didn't.

"Miguel? Miguel?"

The way she mangled his name with her Anglo-inflected pronunciation seemed only more attractive to him then—how she pronounced his name *Mig-well* rather than *Mig-el* sent a tingle through his stomach.

He turned back to them.

Put on his best smile.

Even as he approached Frau Köhler and Mackenzie, Miguel couldn't help but feel that this whole situation couldn't be happening—that it was some fantasy that was only taking place within his imagination. He had met Frau Köhler on more than one occasion, of course, and she had even expressed enthusiasm for his work; she had told him that he was doing *important* work, and he had felt that she wasn't simply providing lip-service . . . he had *felt* that she meant what she'd said.

And Miguel had to admit that he was also struck by Frau Köhler's plans to open up the Moon to those other than the super-rich. To him, at least, it seemed only the right thing to do. But that didn't change the fact that she was his *boss*; and that word somehow sent shivers down his spine no matter how he attempted to qualify it.

When Frau Köhler spoke to him, she spoke directly, meeting his eye.

But there was no sense that she was attempting to read his mind—that she was exercising some kind of *power* over him; an effect which so many of Miguel's past bosses had so obviously attempted to achieve. No, Miguel couldn't help but catch the impression that there was no need for her to read his mind. She already *knew* just what he was thinking.

"What a wonderful display you made," Frau Köhler said.

Miguel was caught wrong-footed for a moment.

And then he recalled the holographic model he had knocked up ahead of the wedding.

He made some bashful remark about it being 'nothing'.

Frau Köhler only smiled back at him.

Then she said something which truly caught his attention.

"I must say," she said, "that I am *most* envious of the opportunity presented to you by Gofreddo. The chance to push back the frontiers of human knowledge; to work on mapping the stars."

Miguel shifted a glance at Mackenzie—feeling caught in two minds.

Although he knew Frau Köhler well, or thought he did, he couldn't quite find the strength to voice his *true* opinion on the matter. He couldn't bring himself to express his *doubts* . . . Frau Köhler just sounded so *enthusiastic*.

"Yes," Miguel replied, smiling. "It *is* a great opportunity, isn't it?"

Even as he uttered the words, he knew there was no reason for him to slip Mackenzie a sidelong glance. He could already tell that she was giving him a reproachful look. He had *told* her just how he felt about this proposed 'voyage' . . . he had informed her of the conclusions he had drawn about it. And yet Miguel just continued to stand there. *Smiling.*

Frau Köhler breathed in deeply so that her shoulders dipped and then rose. She looked from Mackenzie to Miguel, then back to Mackenzie again. She gave Mackenzie a wry smile. "You didn't tell me he was *this* good-looking."

And, with that—with Mackenzie blushing all over—Frau Köhler departed the scene with an innocent curtsey.

When Miguel reached up to touch his own cheeks, he could tell that he was suffering just as much as Mackenzie was.

When Mackenzie spoke her voice was far surer—far *flirtier*—

than the blushes blotting her cheeks suggested it might be. "Well," she said, "I guess my secret's out."

Somehow Miguel managed to seize upon his own confidence. "That's the thing with girl talk," he replied. "You have to assume that—at some point—whatever's said is going to come out in the end."

Mackenzie remained quiet.

Still.

Off in the distance, Miguel couldn't help but hear music starting up.

It wasn't anything like the string quartet which had played throughout the ceremony, however.

This was nothing but an electronically driven bass beat.

Mackenzie looked back to him, a slight smile clinging to her lips. "So, are you gonna ask me to dance or what, Miguel?"

Miguel smiled back at her. "It's Mig-*el* not Mig-*well*."

"Mig-*el*, Mig-*well*—whatever you call yourself. Are we going to dance?"

Miguel took a moment as if measuring his response—as if his response *needed* measuring—and then he said, "Absolutely."

ENTERTAINING RHYTHMS

ackenzie soon felt herself becoming lost to the constant *thud* and *throb* of the music.

She wondered when the Dome lights had gone out—when the Dome day had given way to night.

But it *was* night now.

To begin with it was like she had never leaned into Miguel and kissed him at all. The two of them danced almost separately. They marked out their positions; left a decorous gap between them. She wondered if this might be one of the side-effects of there being no readily available alcohol to lubricate awkward social situations such as this one. When Frau Köhler had insinuated—*out loud*—that she and Mackenzie had discussed Miguel as some sort of an 'eligible bachelor' she had thought that the ground might well open up and swallow her whole.

And then, deciding that the damage had already been done, Mackenzie had seen no reason for her to act coyly in Miguel's presence. So she had asked him to dance.

And here they were.

Several times, as they danced in close vicinity, Mackenzie cast glances in the direction of the bride and groom. As they had been throughout the occasion, they were surrounded by their guests. She hadn't been able to help noticing that Njhay had seemingly become more confident as the ceremony had gone on. He had better eased into himself.

Although Mackenzie could almost physically hear Diane Drake in her ear—telling her that this was something which was *obviously* out of her control . . . something which even micromanagement could never solve—she had to admit that it was a weight off her shoulders to see that Njhay was doing better with the social expectations.

Because, in a way, it *did* feel like her responsibility.

Her responsibility that the bride and groom have their *perfect* wedding.

It was then that Miguel finally made his move.

He took a few steps toward her.

Mackenzie felt her heart strike the back of her throat.

Every muscle in her body stiffened.

"You did a great job," Miguel said.

Although Mackenzie thought that it was something of a wishy-washy comment, she was glad to take a compliment wherever she might find one.

She smiled back at him.

"Thanks," she said. "I think that model of yours really helped things to click into place."

Miguel smiled and shrugged at this—as if it hadn't been anything at all.

Then, apparently on impulse, he leaned in.

Pressed his lips—*hard*—up against hers.

Mackenzie felt a skittish sensation pass across the surface of her skin. She almost forgot herself as Miguel's tongue explored her mouth—she forgot that she was supposed to be offering some sort of resistance. That she was supposed to be kissing him *back*.

And so she did.

With *gusto*.

He gave a moan and she felt the vibrations of it pass through her body—travel right down to the pit of her stomach.

"Shall we . . ." Miguel said, but his words were lost.

Mackenzie grabbed hold of his wrist, dragging him behind her.

They navigated the crowds.

Reached an apparently isolated spot.

Mackenzie threw herself into him.

Kissed him again.

As she squeezed his hand, she could feel him trembling slightly.

She could tell she intimidated him.

And she *liked* it.

Although she was conscious of the celebrations continuing without her—that there were no doubt things happening which she should've been supervising—she knew that she couldn't allow this situation to slip through her fingers.

Not now.

Not *ever*.

She led Miguel in through a gap in the bushes, and to a quiet spot.

They were enclosed—on all sides—by the foliage.

The gentle bass continued to throb away.

It felt as if her heart was attempting to match the beat.

And getting carried away.

Punching harder and harder and harder.

She grabbed Miguel by the hand, twisting him around so that

she could get a better look at him in the near-darkness of the Dome night-time.

She saw the light flash off the surface of his eyes.

And the slight glistening of moisture on his lower lip.

It was now or never.

Again acting on instinct—that was all she seemed to possess now—she reached up, placing her palms hard against his chest. She pushed him firmly. Watched him trip backward.

He caught his fall with his hands.

Landed on the soft grass below.

Unwilling to allow him a moment's respite, she clambered on top of him. She perched on his stomach—a leg on either side of his flanks. She stared into his eyes, feeling her power.

Feeling that she *dominated* him completely.

She felt the heat of his skin up against her own.

And she could breathe in the gentle scent of champagne and grass on the air.

The bass beat urged her onward.

She reached for his trousers.

Gently drew them down.

There was no need for her to *push* her strength on him now.

She had made him understand that she was in control.

And that was enough.

As he strained to kiss her, she allowed her fingertips to trace the outline of his neck; the tattoo which continued beneath the collar of his shirt.

She raised her eyebrows.

"You know," she said. "I always wanted to see that tattoo of yours."

She felt him tremble slightly.

She wondered if she might've crossed a line.

No—she was in control.

He would do what she told him.

What she *willed* him to do.

As gently as she had removed his trousers, Mackenzie worked at the buttons of Miguel's shirt collar. And then she removed the tie. When she had shrugged his jacket off, she turned her attention to the rest of the shirt buttons—undoing each and every one. Then, with a single, swift action, she gripped hold of his flanks and used all her strength to flip him over.

At the same time, she couldn't help but acknowledge that he aided her—making his body limp so that she might mould it to her desire.

When he lay face down, his bare back exposed, she took in the tattoo. It was elaborate—*far* more elaborate than she would've imagined. When she thought later about her expectations, she realised that she had anticipated a snake or a scorpion or a tiger . . . something threatening to be inked onto his back. However, she hadn't been prepared for that which *was* there.

The tattoo featured a mangy dog in a side alley.

It was snarling.

Eyes wild—*crazed*.

A full moon beamed in the background.

Mackenzie traced the lines which'd been inked onto Miguel's skin. She was aware of her mouth falling ajar as she did so and was glad there was nobody nearby watching. She supposed she must've looked like a ditz, or else like some naïve *virgin* rendered thunder-struck by her first sight of Real-Life Man Flesh.

When she spoke again, there was none of the raw passion which'd led her to bringing Miguel here—to snatching him away from the party as quickly as she could. Her words were measured. She supposed that she *must* sound somewhat naïve.

"What does it mean?" she asked.

Miguel noticeably recoiled beneath her touch.

But Mackenzie wasn't about to let him loose.

Not *yet*.

If they were to go . . . *further* . . . then she was determined to know what she was getting herself in for. If Miguel had skeletons lurking at the back of his closet then she was going to know them.

She was determined.

She knew that she needed to be patient—so she waited for her answer.

And finally it came.

"It is a part of my history," Miguel said, finally, his voice slightly muffled because he was lying face down . . . and because Mackenzie was sat upon his back. "Something that I escaped from . . . but something which I shall never escape from—if you understand my meaning."

She couldn't help but be brought in mind of her raw ambition —of that drive which seemed to tower over each and *every* thing she did . . . that voice, the one which Diane Drake had expressed, the one which told her that she needed to continue to challenge herself.

That was the only way to self-improvement.

The one and only method which would work.

She would never leave *that* behind.

Not until she came across a challenge big enough to occupy her ego . . .

Finally, feeling her raw passion relenting, and a woozier, warmer sense beginning to overcome her, she let off her weight, rolling her legs away from his spine.

On her knees—not caring about bringing her dress into contact with the grass—she peered at him sidelong. It was strange to see him from another angle. To *not* see him straight on.

To see him *beside* her.

"I think I understand just what you're saying," she replied, with a smile.

Then she reached her arms out to his throat.

Clasping his chin in her hands.

She was as delicate as she could manage. She used the grinding bass beat to guide her. She felt as if she was riding sea currents—as if she had been instantly transported back down to Earth . . . as if she had been stranded in the middle of the sea in nothing but a flimsy raft made up out of flotsam.

And she had this hunk of man with her.

She had *Miguel* with her.

Her tenderness surprised her. It was a quality which she had never expected. She had always thought of men as she imagined they often must think of women:

A *conquest*.

But Miguel was different.

She felt no appetite.

No driving desire to *consume* him.

She wanted to enjoy the sensations.

As she ran her hands over his tight, well-muscled abdomen, she felt his heartbeat.

It was rapid.

Like her own.

She felt his warm breath brush up against her skin.

It brought all the hairs to a standing position.

As the bass beat in the distance continued to grind away—as it reached a climax of some sort—Mackenzie could feel that she was doing the same with Miguel.

That they were arriving *together*.

And it was wonderful.

TERMINATE FESTIVITIES

arolin Köhler stood to one extreme of the dance floor. She observed the dancers all moving together to the music. As she felt the rhythmic bass track flood over her, she couldn't help but turn her gaze upward—to the darkness of space which dwelled above.

All those profundities just waiting to be discovered.

She wondered how mankind had allowed itself to become so distracted; with wars, with politics, with *money* . . . those were all like games—*toys*—when compared to all that was out there ready to be discovered.

If only one had the courage.

As she felt the little champagne she had imbibed make her drowsy, she decided that it was well past her bedtime. True it was still a way off midnight—before the time when the bride and groom would be wished off on their way to bed—but this *was* her Dome, after all; and she could break with social niceties when she saw fit.

Right as she turned away from the dancers, and toward the landing pad where a queue of PEARs was already accumulating, she noticed movement in the bushes.

A pair of figures approaching.

Returning to the dance floor.

She could tell who they were merely from their silhouettes.

Mackenzie Angliss.

Miguel Cruz.

She absorbed their glowing cheeks—how their clothes were slightly rumpled and how Mackenzie seemed suddenly preoccupied about combing her fingers through her hair.

Karolin smiled wide and long. She felt a warmth pass through her bloodstream. It appeared that—following their chat—Mackenzie had decided to come down on one side of the fence.

She had broken through that paranoid notion that Gofreddo and the others were attempting to *nudge* her and Miguel together . . . she had decided—instead—to follow her heart.

Unbeknownst to the couple, she continued to observe them as they re-joined the other dancers. The two of them glanced about, apparently gauging whether or not their absence had been noted.

It *had* been noted. If only by Karolin.

But she wouldn't tell a soul.

She turned her attention away, centring her gaze back on the happy couple—Louise and Njhay—as they danced together, the two of them beaming at one another.

With a slight sigh, Karolin laid the glass of fizzy water down on a nearby table and made her way out through the guests to the landing pad. As she observed the PEAR descending toward her—ready to whisk her back to the Blue Moon Suite—she couldn't help but feel a profound happiness soar through her.

Although she was living out the last moments of her existence, she didn't feel sad—not even nostalgic. She was pleased only to live in the present. To absorb every last detail which life had to give her. Before surrendering to death.

23

CLEAN-UP OPERATION

*M*ackenzie took in the *Crescent Gardens* with the early-morning light.

The early-morning *Dome* lights.

It was about what she had expected. There were dirty glasses aplenty. The grass had been well trodden. And there was—she couldn't help noticing—a bra hanging off the back of a nearby chair.

She stood for a few moments, just studying the scene. She watched on as the cleaning droids and drones went about their work. As they plucked rubbish off the floors; as the droids reluctantly went to work on the trampled lawns with their hydration tools and all those other functions which she barely understood.

It was a strange few moments. She felt almost as if she was the only person present on the Moon. As if she had—*somehow*—jetted herself up here solo. And now she was taking in the evidence left behind by the long-gone colonists.

The fact that she had woken up beside a gorgeous man bore no correlation with her rapidity in leaving the bed behind to come and check on the state of the Crescent Gardens.

She had always been an early-riser. And, worse than that, once she had woken up she found it almost impossible to drift back off to sleep. This attribute had frustrated former lovers and boyfriends who all—*apparently*—pined for the romantic ideal of 'kissing her awake'.

She didn't know exactly how Miguel would take her absence.

She supposed it would be another test; if she chose to see it that way.

It wasn't just that she would wake up and be unable to return to sleep, either. It had more to do with how her mind would suddenly wind into action, her thoughts becoming obsessed with the day which lay ahead. And she could do nothing but leap into action herself and go about solving all the problems facing her. And that was what she was doing now.

She knew—better than anyone—that the Crescent Gardens needed to be open to the clientele in a couple of hours' time, and she wasn't about to allow them to witness all the debauchery this scene implied. However, she had to admit that the droids and drones were doing a good job of cleaning things up. There wasn't much for her to tweak . . . although she did find *certain* things.

Seeing that the drone assigned to trimming and pruning the lawns was leaving some patches of grass a *touch* flattened, she ordered it to leave a little more length.

And then she observed a droid collecting rubbish which had neglected the stem of a broken champagne glass, half concealed beneath a bush.

She actually bent down and deposited the broken stem in the droid's receptacle herself . . . no one could honestly say she wasn't a 'hands-on' manager . . .

Once she had given the Gardens a once-over and decided that there was nothing for her to do for the time being—that everything seemed to be, if not currently in good order, then soon to be so—she took a stroll through the Celestial Gardens labs.

When she passed by Njhay Garcia's lab, she took the opportunity to duck inside and poke about. She didn't believe that he would be coming into the office early today, if he came in at all.

Contrary to popular belief—about her only being interested in the 'commercial' aspects of the Celestial Stays Dome—she always liked to know what was going on all over the place.

Although it might stun Njhay to realise, she actually had a decent grasp on what he was currently studying . . . at least when it came to the *broad* strokes.

She started off with the microscope, instantly observing—as was Njhay's carefree way—that he had left a slide locked in place. She leaned over the device and peered through the eyeholes.

All she made out were colourful blurs.

Although she imagined that—to Njhay—these colourful blurs were nothing short of *fascinating*, she could only draw limited meaning from them. So she moved onto something a little more concrete. The log screen he had left on.

As with all screens, this one floated in mid-air.

She stood before it, taking in the various charts, graphs and timers running. She could see that Njhay was measuring temperature and the percentage of some chemical makeup or other. And that he was also tracking something to do with 'solar strength'.

She was on the point of again moving on from this particular partition of Njhay's studies when something about the screen caught her eye.

Even on second glance, she wasn't entirely sure what it was—what *had* caught her eye.

And then she caught sight of it.

Off to the corner of the screen, there was a folder which was labelled—not particularly confidentially—'Gofreddo Trip'.

With an eye roll, she casually made a flicking gesture at the screen which relegated the graphs and readings to a minimised window. She selected the folder and opened it up.

Within the folder, she found a variety of things.

Among them were dry, technical lists, ones which she supposed Njhay had developed by some sort of scientific method—the various things he hoped to investigate during the voyage.

What caught her eye more, however, was the hyperlink leading to correspondence surrounding the trip. She frowned briefly. Then ordered it open.

Being the scatterbrain he was, Njhay hadn't thought to protect the correspondence with either encryption or a password. The messages featured a back-and-forth between Njhay Garcia and Gofreddo Zito. Most of the messages were on-point—even *dryly* so.

From what Mackenzie could garner from the conversations, Gofreddo had appointed—or *would appoint*—Njhay as the Ship's Scientist. It actually made her smile to see the various messages which Njhay had sent Gofreddo with wildly detailed plans of what he would do once on-board the Zito Express—or whatever they were planning on Christening the ship.

There was what she believed constituted something like proposals for funding back on Earth.

All that would follow these lengthy missives, however, was a single-word response from Gofreddo's end:

Okay.

On the brink of backing out of Njhay's correspondence, she couldn't help but come grinding to a halt when she saw her own name mentioned in one of the messages to Gofreddo.

She did a double-take, unsure that she had read what she had just read.

Then she went back and read over:

. . . I must insist that you reconsider Mackenzie for the mission—I do not believe that she would be conducive to the team. She could well be a disruptive influence. Then again, should you choose to go down the route of inviting her aboard it would, of course, in no way affect my interest in the mission. As I have already stated, I believe this to be the great opportunity of our times. Certainly from a scientific perspective.

Mackenzie then looked to Gofreddo's reply, seeing—with a smile on her lips—him beating away Njhay's concerns. She was actually quite humbled at how glowing Gofreddo was about her character; about how she would be an '*invaluable* asset' to the crew. How her integrity was 'unsurpassable' . . . and then the irony hit Mackenzie; that spying on Njhay's personal correspondence was hardly becoming of someone with 'unsurpassable' integrity . . .

And she *would* have broken off reading there if it hadn't been for her eyes accidentally skimming over the message which followed.

She traced the name several times, unsure that she had quite grasped the gravity of the situation.

It was a response from Miguel.

As if she was about to get caught, she glanced up and looked around.

There was, of course, no one nearby.

No one to discover her.

So she read on.

And wasn't quite certain she believed what she read.

Obviously solicited by Njhay, Miguel's response—point by point—detailed just why Mackenzie would be nothing short of an unmitigated disaster to have on board the ship.

It was only when Mackenzie reached the bottom of Miguel's message that she realised some tears had snuck free of the corners of her eyes. She reached up and wiped them clear from her cheeks. She blinked several times, brought the screen before her a little clearer.

It was difficult to take the message as a cohesive whole.

Individual words and phrases from Miguel's message hung in her mind's eye:

Manipulative.
Difficult to work with.
Controlling.
Condescending.
Overwhelmingly ambitious.
Domineering.
Heartless.
Frigid.

. . . Okay, after last night, Mackenzie couldn't help but sniff a reluctant laugh at *that* particular comment . . . but the list went on:

Easily distracted.
Hard to please.
Demanding.

Mackenzie's heart hung in her throat.

Of course she had enough self-awareness to see truth in these qualities, and yet that didn't make it any easier for her to read them; to consciously sift through each and every one.

She thought about what Diane Drake would've said of these words.

About how it was never a successful business person's goal to be 'liked' . . . the key, as Diane had always drummed into Mackenzie, was to establish 'rapport'—*rapport* greased the wheels of business the world-around.

Mackenzie looked over the date of the message.

It was the day after Gofreddo had invited her and Miguel onto the crew.

She supposed that Njhay had wanted to get his criticisms in early.

He had wanted to introduce the concept that Gofreddo *shouldn't*—under any circumstances!—allow Mackenzie on board the ship as quickly as possible.

Allow the idea some time to mature; to grow legs.

And Miguel had agreed with him.

Even though it seemed as if her and Miguel's relationship had moved *far* beyond the initial observations, as he laid them out in the message to Gofreddo, she couldn't help but feel a slight burning sensation in her gut.

Was it even possible for someone's point of view to shift so rapidly and emphatically?

Finished with her self-torture, she backed away from the screen, at the same time shutting down the layers of correspondence which were open to her.

It was time to get back to work.

24

MEDIA SPECULATION

t was later on that same day when Mackenzie received an urgent summons for her to attend the *Lunar Landings* newsroom.

When Mackenzie turned up at the Armstrong Archive—and to the *Lunar Landings* newsroom—everything seemed to be far more manic than usual.

That was to say that people seemed to be pouring out of every available door.

Each and every surface available appeared to be occupied by someone beavering away.

Mackenzie waded through them all, arriving before Kyra who seemed to be equally occupied as the rest.

Kyra glanced up briefly. "Thought this was going to be a nice, quiet day too, huh? That we'd just get the chance to sleep off our hangovers—be able to drift through the shift?"

Although Mackenzie hadn't thought anything of the sort—she

never *had* been able to think that way—she couldn't help but nod by way of reply.

The old reflexive habit of establishing 'rapport' was alive and well with her.

"What's wrong?" Mackenzie asked.

Kyra averted her gaze a moment. She bellowed something across the newsroom to an unseen employee. When she turned back, her expression was grim. "Seems there's been a leak."

"A 'leak'?"

"Uh-huh," Kyra muttered.

"What do you mean a leak?"

"I mean," Kyra said, gradually turning her attention back to Mackenzie, "that someone has caught wind of Gofreddo's plans." She dropped her voice several levels, apparently realising the irony of what she was saying in a newsroom—with journalists all around. "And that Frau Köhler has made the trip up here."

Mackenzie paused for a second, assessing the situation. Then she said, "But isn't that okay—I mean, we weren't *planning* on keeping this secret forever. We were going to have to say something *sometime* . . ."

She waited a few moments, realising that Kyra was busy with the Link; that she had her finger pressed to her earpiece issuing some command or communicating with someone.

When Kyra was paying her attention again, Mackenzie continued, "It's just Gofreddo we're waiting on, isn't it? I mean, we need his go-ahead for us to reveal the details of the mission."

Kyra's expression was stonelike now. She eyed Mackenzie closely. "And Gofreddo's waiting on you and Miguel to make your minds up—so we can publish the crew details."

Here, despite herself, Mackenzie felt warmth surge to her

cheeks. She attempted to conceal the reaction by turning her head away. When she got through with acting like a schoolgirl—as she admonished herself—she shifted her attention back to Kyra. "You're saying that now's the time?" Mackenzie asked. "That it's on *us*?"

Kyra shook her head. "No, what I'm saying is that we can cover this up but—*sooner or later*—the truth is going to come out." She paused, once more pressing her finger against her earpiece. "And I won't be held personally responsible for spreading misinformation."

A flush of anger passed through Mackenzie.

She turned her back on Kyra and stormed away.

And people had the nerve to call *her* arrogant!

Despite the night they'd spent together the previous evening, Mackenzie was hardly in the mood to bump into Miguel. She didn't want to have to awkwardly explain why she had *disappeared* when he'd woken up. She knew—from experience—that it worked best for her to avoid confrontations with men. She always had to have the last word . . . she always had to emerge from whatever argument as the winner. Uh-oh, was that her self-awareness showing again?

Although she didn't know the internal layout of the Armstrong Archive all that intuitively, she managed to navigate through the sprawling, labyrinthine corridors where she came upon what turned out to be a back door. She let herself out, already feeling the fresh Dome air hitting her cheeks. Making her feel like a new woman.

It was as she was rounding the building of the Archive itself when she almost walked—*bang!*—straight into Miguel Cruz.

It appeared that he was just as shaken up by their encounter as she was.

For several seconds, the two of them just stood there, regarding one another, in silence.

Finally—*awkwardly*—he leaned forward to kiss her on the cheek.

She allowed him to kiss her, but not without a slight flinch.

He seemed to sense her discomfort because he backed up several steps, giving her the space which she clearly needed.

"Uh, hi," he said, breaking the silence between them, and scratching at his neck as he did so . . . as if she might still be thinking about his naked body and *that* tattoo which was inked onto his back.

To tell the truth, she was . . . among other *distinctive* features.

Even though she had told herself absolutely *not* to apologise to anyone—for any reason—she couldn't help saying, "I'm sorry for disappearing this morning." She caught something of her former swagger, managing to give a nonchalant shrug. "Duty calls, you know?"

He gave her a slight smile, but she could tell that he was feeling just as awkward as she was. He looked away from her, to some indistinct spot outside the Dome on the lunar plains. "It was . . . I . . . didn't expect . . ."

Mackenzie managed to get herself back together. "Look," she said. "I'm running late—I have to *go*." And then she made to pass him by; to go and catch a PEAR.

She could really do with a shower, if not a swim also.

Miguel murmured something. Then, seemingly unable to prevent her from leaving, he reached out and seized hold of the sleeve of her overalls.

Mackenzie had no option but to turn around and face up to

him. If she'd had her wits better about her maybe she would've attempted to shrug off his grip. But she had to admit that she *was* suffering somewhat from the night before.

"I . . . just wanted you to know," he began. "That last night . . ."

But she was already shaking her head.

Tears pricked her eyes.

"Last night was nothing," she replied.

Now she did find the strength to squirm free of his grip.

Miguel didn't insist.

Looking him in the eye—no longer caring that he saw her so vulnerable—she said, "It was just the moment—it was just the *situation* . . . all these crazy *plans*, you know."

Miguel gave her a wide-eyed stare, as if he had no idea what she was talking about.

She decided to make things easier for him.

"Listen," she said. "I don't think that this voyage—*space exploration*—is for me. I don't think that it was *ever* for me." She gave a grim smile. "All I've ever known, all that I know *now*, is people, other human beings." She paused, wondering how best she might be able to put it. "*Earth.*"

Although she wished, more than anything, to break free of him, to go catch a PEAR back to the Basements—to be *alone* for a while —she couldn't bring herself to merely walk away.

She had always believed in clean breaks.

She had always believed that it was better not to leave things *unsaid* . . . that might lead to resentment. And resentment—apart from anything else—was bad for business.

"I saw what you said about me," she said. "In those messages between you and Gofreddo and *Njhay.*" She made sure to stress Njhay's name as if it was a swearword.

Miguel just stood dim-witted—*stunned* even.

"You don't *want* me on that ship," she said. "You don't *want* me there." She arched her shoulders, flashed her eyebrows, and then added, her voice cracking now, "So why *lie* about it?"

Miguel parted his lips slightly, but no sound emerged.

Mackenzie gave him another few seconds and—when he said nothing at all—she turned her back on him and walked away. She caught the first PEAR off the landing pad.

Once the Armstrong Archive was out of sight, she burst into tears.

25

RESEARCH PRIVILEGES

*M*iguel *watched Mackenzie's PEAR* slip from view. He felt as if invisible pins danced across the surface of his skin. He could feel his whole body rigid—every last muscle drawn taut. His heart was beating thickly and evenly against the underside of his throat.

It might've been better if he had had the chance to speculate as to what might have gone wrong; as to the reason for Mackenzie's reaction.

But she had spelled it out to him in clear terms.

She had told him that she had seen those messages he'd shared with Gofreddo and Njhay.

The ones in which he had added weight to Njhay's argument that Mackenzie would be an unfit crewmember. He would've liked to say that they hadn't been true—that he hadn't said those things —but that would've made him a liar.

Miguel had always seen himself—everything else apart—as someone who was honest. As someone who didn't unnecessarily bend or omit the truth. He couldn't help but feel slightly guilty that he had failed to validate Mackenzie's claims emphatically.

He should've *confirmed* those things he'd said.

And then they could've gone from there.

He might've added certain qualifiers—or *attempted* to.

He would've said that—*since* he had said those things—his opinion toward Mackenzie had changed dramatically; that those surface attributes which he had mentioned in the communication with Gofreddo and Njhay were just that. They were all factors he had spotted while looking on from afar. Before he had got to know her better.

Before *last night* . . .

It was only after he had been standing on the spot, continuing to stare on after Mackenzie's PEAR, that he realised the reason why he had been unable to say anything to Mackenzie.

He knew that he had *wanted* to tell her that she was wrong; that she *would* be a good fit for the journey into Outer Space.

But that would've simply been a lie.

There was nothing more important in reality to Miguel than making decisions or forming opinions based on evidence—and all the evidence he had seen thus far pointed only to a single conclusion: that in a situation such as the one they were facing, Mackenzie would be nothing but trouble.

All of the studies had shown—time and time again—that those who sought to impress their beliefs, or their superiority, on others would only succeed in breeding resentment.

In the end, it was nothing personal.

She just didn't fit the profile.

Throughout their face-off, Miguel had been all too aware that he didn't have much of a place when it came to speaking about whether or not Mackenzie should accept the offer to join Gofreddo's crew. After all, he himself was still unsure whether it was entirely advisable to put himself at the mercy of such a strong personality as Gofreddo Zito.

Sure, his motives were 'pure' or 'noble' but that didn't work either in favour of—or against—his capacities as the Captain, or whatever title he had in mind to take on for this voyage.

Miguel didn't fit the profile for a crewmember *either*.

If only—in her apparent spy efforts—Mackenzie had continued to scan through the conversation to the part where Miguel had discounted himself as a good selection for the crew, then she might've seen his logical processes in action.

But it seemed that he had already failed.

And now she was angry with him.

With a sigh, he shifted away from the lunar plains, and turned back to the Archive.

He had a whole heap of studying to get done.

Despite himself he hadn't managed to get the offer out of his head . . . he hadn't managed to definitively say that what Gofreddo Zito had planned was maniacal.

And that rankled.

26

ROLE INTERCHANGE

arolin Köhler had accepted Mackenzie Angliss's request to meet with her as soon as she had received it. Of course, she already understood Mackenzie's plans, that whatever she eventually decided about accepting or declining the place on Gofreddo Zito's spaceship, she would be leaving Celestial Stays at the end of the current rotation.

Karolin didn't begrudge Mackenzie this, of course, she knew that often the very best of her employees strove to break free and go off on their own.

What appeared to attract people to working on the Moon in the first place was a sense of adventure, a sense of having nothing left to lose . . . and—more often than not—loneliness.

To Karolin's mind, Mackenzie ticked all three of these attributes. And so it was no wonder that she yearned to be turned free; that she wished to strike out on some new path.

On her *next* adventure.

They had agreed to meet here—in the Blue Moon Suite.

That had been Karolin's request.

As she sat in one of the armchairs by the window, she couldn't help absentmindedly gazing down at her exposed forearm, and seeing the giveaway blotchy mark there.

When the Link informed her that there was someone at the door, she rolled her sleeve back down—to cover the mark—and accepted the request for entrance.

Mackenzie Angliss walked in through the doorway.

Karolin rose out of her seat, feeling as if her bones themselves were aching. She managed to pin on a smile all the same. To greet Mackenzie with something resembling *enthusiasm*.

Karolin supposed it was something like absentmindedness which was down to her not noticing who was in Mackenzie's company right away; that it was Charlie Cuevo, Mackenzie's personal assistant, and the one who Mackenzie had recommended be her replacement.

Karolin gestured the two women down into the armchairs which stood opposite her.

They did as she suggested.

With the two women settled into their seats, Karolin cracked another smile and looked them over. "I suppose there shall be some *big* changes happening here."

"Yes," Mackenzie replied. "It seems so."

Karolin looked over at Charlie. "And from everything that Mackenzie has told me, you are really quite a capable young woman."

Charlie smiled back at Karolin, inclining her head.

Despite Charlie's stolid outward appearance, Karolin could tell that there was a certain tenderness beneath the surface; a sort of *sensibility*.

Karolin recalled how in earlier days—back when she'd been

more ambitious, and *far* more naïve—she would've called such a quality *weakness* . . .

Karolin looked to Mackenzie, and then to Charlie. It was really on a whim that she decided it was best for her to level with these two women; to inform them of her decision. If she was going to trust them with her vision for Celestial Stays then it only followed that she should *also* trust in them what the immediate future would hold.

"I have agreed—with Gofreddo Zito—to travel on his ship."

Karolin slumped back in the armchair, analysing the women's reaction.

First she noticed Charlie's gaping mouth, and how she leaned forward in the armchair.

She seemed to forget her timid nature for a moment, saying, "But—*Frau Köhler!*—I do not understand!"

Karolin shifted a glance at Mackenzie, whose expression was far more measured.

Although Karolin wouldn't have liked to speculate, she wouldn't have been surprised if Mackenzie had second-guessed her . . . if she had known just what Karolin intended to do.

Mackenzie was so after her own heart.

Karolin turned back to Charlie—the woman who would be Mackenzie's successor. "It is not a decision which I have taken lightly, as I am sure you shall both appreciate."

Neither woman said anything.

Then Charlie spoke again. "But, Frau Köhler, what shall become of the Celestial Stays Dome without you?"

"*Karolin*, please," she said, then continued, "I have already put in place all of the plans I have for the Dome, and it shall be Mackenzie's successor's charge to see them through." She gave a shrug. "Or to readjust them as is seen fit."

"Oh, Frau Köhler," Charlie replied, still leaning forward in her armchair. "I would not think to change *your* plans."

This was what Karolin had been afraid of.

But she made no outward display of having proven herself right about something.

"You have no need to worry," Karolin said. "I have already taken measures—put together a council—which shall ensure that all the correct decisions are made with respect to the Dome. To ensure that the community—those on *Earth*—are permitted to continue visiting the Moon. So that the adventure will not be forgotten."

Karolin again cast a glance in Mackenzie's direction, hoping that she might take the opportunity to speak up. Even after all these years, Karolin was keen to hear the opinions of those she respected. And she certainly respected Mackenzie.

However, it was Charlie again who spoke up.

Her expression was almost goggle-eyed.

"And you are not *afraid* . . . of the mission into Outer Space?"

Karolin gave a shrug and then a slight sigh. "Well, yes," she replied. "But it would be more concerning if I was *not* afraid—that would mean that there is no adventure for me to discover. That I have *tired* of exploring."

Mouth agape, Charlie turned her attention onto Mackenzie, and then back to Karolin. However, before Charlie had a chance to say anything more, Mackenzie had the good sense to speak up herself.

"I appreciate your decision, *Karolin*," Mackenzie said.

Karolin couldn't help but think that this might well be the first time that Mackenzie had addressed her by her first name without prompting.

Mackenzie continued, "And I am sure it will be a *wonderful* experience—"

Although Karolin had made it something of a personal credo of hers not to interrupt people, she couldn't help but make an exception in this case. "You are not going?" she asked, head tilted to one side, not bothering to hide her surprise.

Mackenzie coloured slightly. She glanced to Charlie, who looked equally surprised—perhaps she hadn't yet heard about Zito's voyage. Finally, Mackenzie looked back at Karolin. "I don't think it'd be the right thing for me," she replied, then shrugged, as if she was explaining away some sort of bugbear. "I guess I'm just more of an Earth sort of girl."

Karolin was well aware that she was glowering. And yet she couldn't think of anything else to do. She couldn't *prevent* herself from being totally taken off guard by what it was that Mackenzie had said. Remembering herself, Karolin looked to Charlie, then smiled. "Would you mind leaving us alone for a few moments?"

Charlie looked surprised but she got up out of her seat without any delay, trod toward the door.

When the door had shut behind her, Karolin supposed she was glad to have escaped the situation.

Karolin turned her attention back to Mackenzie. "The other night," she said. "I thought I saw . . ."

But—as so often seemed to be the case—Mackenzie anticipated her. "Miguel is just a friend," she replied. "And if it was . . . *something more* . . . well, I don't think that I possess the required faith to *throw* myself into a situation with him. A situation from which neither of us would ever be able to escape."

" 'Escape' ?" Karolin couldn't help echoing.

Mackenzie nodded along. "Maybe to some it sounds romantic —flying off into the stars—but, to me, it just seems like it's . . . I dunno . . . a little *crazy*."

Karolin absorbed this argument for several moments. She

brought her knuckle up to her mouth and suckled on the nib. It was a bad habit which she'd had since school. Everybody had failed to relieve her of it: teachers, parents . . . nobody had had any measure of success. And now Karolin supposed that it was too late to stop doing it; too late for it to *matter*, in any case.

"Do you not think that—throughout the ages—all true explorers have felt this way? Do you not consider that *others* have felt *fearful?*" Although Karolin often had to chide herself to keep personal belief out of her arguments—especially in a somewhat professional context—she found that it was impossible here. "What would have become of the world if everyone had stayed in exactly the same place they started? What discoveries *wouldn't* have been made?"

Mackenzie's eyes remained locked on Karolin's.

Karolin felt a throbbing sensation pass through her lungs.

It was either time for her next round of medication or she felt that whatever effort she was exerting in convincing Mackenzie was falling by the wayside.

On impulse, Karolin leaned forward, perching on the edge of her armchair. She reached out for Mackenzie's hands, took hold of them.

Mackenzie trembled slightly when she did, but Karolin was unwilling to allow her grip to be anything but strong—*insistent*.

"You *must* do this," Karolin said. "This is the greatest opportunity of our age—and you are *perfect* for the challenge."

Mackenzie glanced up at her briefly.

Her eyes seemed almost to *burn* in their sockets.

When Mackenzie spoke again, there was a vulnerability in her voice.

Indeed, she spoke almost in a whisper.

"They don't want me," Mackenzie said. "For the mission, I mean."

Karolin thought about pressing Mackenzie for more information but she was fairly certain that she could garner sufficient information from Mackenzie's touch. From the way that her strength itself appeared almost to be fading.

"Ah," Karolin finally replied, "*Jealousy.*"

27

COMMUNITY SERVICE

*P*atrick *Fourie* yanked hard on the controls of the Lunar
Shuttle, straightening it out following the latest loop-
the-loop. Just like the children who packed out the Shuttle, Patrick
wore a wide grin.

It took almost all of Mackenzie's strength to raise even the
slightest of smiles.

In fact, she felt almost detached from the excitement which
buzzed all around her. She felt as if the children who were packed
into the Lunar Shuttle were acting on some other plane of existence. She wondered if it *was* just youthful exuberance. That beautiful innocence which dwelled in each and every soul before the
world's crushing force made itself felt.

They were passing over the Lunar One Monument right now.

Mackenzie peered out through the glass as it passed by.

As she always did, she felt moved by the sight, to know that all
those people—all those *explorers*, as Frau Köhler had put it—had

died so that they might push back the frontiers of human experience. So that they might *better* mankind.

Was that who Mackenzie was?

Was she an *explorer*?

The others certainly didn't seem to think so . . . although Frau Köhler's school teacher-like comment about how the others were just 'jealous' had appealed to Mackenzie somewhat.

Several times throughout the trip, Patrick Fourie glanced over his shoulder at her.

She wanted—more than anything—to tell him to *stop* looking . . . but it was so obvious that what he was doing was innocuous—that he was *concerned* for her—she knew it was impossible to say anything at all.

Patrick was bringing the Shuttle back toward the Dome, and, more specifically, the Hangar.

Mackenzie watched on as the Dome loomed large; as the Shuttle Hangar appeared almost like the gaping mouth of some lunar beast. She wondered about the times when humans had believed that there were creatures living on the Moon; mystical beings . . . *Moonmen* . . . well, the only *Moonmen* present here were the employees and clientele of Celestial Stays . . .

As Patrick brought the Shuttle in through the Hangar doors, and neatly down onto its assigned landing pad, Mackenzie was aware of the children all bouncing up off their seats, casting away their chest straps with a flinging motion.

She glanced back at Patrick—again catching his eye.

Almost apart from the two of them, the children filed their way off the Shuttle, down the rapidly opening steps, and to the minders from Hospitality who were awaiting them.

Patrick and Mackenzie watched on as the excitable children

were herded away to the landing pad where several PEARs queued up waiting for them.

When the two of them were alone, Patrick spoke up.

"Never gets old, does it?"

"Mmm?" Mackenzie replied, turning back to him. "Oh," she said, "you mean with the *kids?*"

Patrick smiled. "You were another world away, huh?"

His smile was infectious, and she couldn't help returning the favour. "Yeah," she replied. "I suppose you could say that."

Patrick nodded to the children as the last of them disappeared off through the doors of the Hangar. Several of them waved to him and he waved back. He looked to Mackenzie once more. "It's so easy to get used to things here," he said. "I mean, it's great when these kids come up here, when they get to see the celestial body they've seen up in the sky their whole lives. Kind of works like a reminder for us, too—reminds us that this isn't normal; that we're not living *normal* lives."

Mackenzie thought on the children. They were part of one of the many 'community' programmes which Frau Köhler had recently been putting into place. She supposed that this was something of the legacy which she had alluded to in their previous meeting; during the meeting in which Frau Köhler had informed Mackenzie and Charlie that she too would be travelling on Gofreddo Zito's spaceship. And in the same meeting during which Mackenzie had revealed that she *wouldn't* be travelling. She was unsure why she had picked that exact moment to say that she wouldn't, and she hadn't told anyone else aside from Frau Köhler. Somehow that made it less real.

It made Mackenzie's decision less real.

In actual fact, Mackenzie wouldn't have made her decision

until she had told Gofreddo directly to his face. But that would take tact—a strategy.

Gofreddo had a nasty habit of being extremely *convincing* when he wanted to be.

Finally, Mackenzie turned back to Patrick. "But this *is* our normal life," she said. "This is what we *do* for a living. Don't you think that it's just part of the process that the wonder becomes jaded? That things aren't as bright and *sparkly* as they once were?"

Patrick breathed in deeply then sighed out. He laid his forearms across the console before him and looked out to the lunar plains. "It's kind of like getting older, isn't it? I wish I could still be that kid—like those that we took out today . . . I wish I could forget everything that I know."

Mackenzie appreciated this thought for several seconds, and then something occurred to her. She slipped Patrick a sidelong glance. "Why do you think Gofreddo wants me to go along on the mission? What does he think I can give . . . you know . . . other than just bossing people around?"

Mackenzie expected Patrick to blow her off with some clichéd response about how she was a 'good person' or how she had some skill or other which would be required for the mission.

However, to her surprise, his response was candid.

"I don't know," he replied. "Just like I don't know why he picked *me* for the mission." He shrugged. "I don't know why he picked *any* of us—why didn't he go through some more rigorous selection protocol back on Earth? There're surely way more people down there who'd be infinitely more suited to the task."

Mackenzie allowed his response to fill her ears.

And then she said, "So?"

Patrick hunched his shoulders and gave a slight sigh. "Maybe

Gofreddo just wanted to jet off into space with his friends? Perhaps he just thought that we all *fit together* well?"

Mackenzie thought on this for a moment or two, and then said, "Does Gofreddo think of me as a 'friend'?"

Patrick gave her an odd look, then he smirked. "Of course he does—isn't it obvious?"

Mackenzie stewed on this then looked back off through the Hangar windows to the lunar plains.

And she wondered if—where humans were concerned—there was anything at all which was 'obvious'.

28

ORGANISED OFF-DUTY PERIOD

ackenzie surprised herself when she arrived outside Miguel's room in the Basements. This was where she had woken several nights previously—following Njhay and Louise's wedding. She supposed that her brain had been on some sort of auto-pilot. It had been her feet which'd seemingly taken on a life of their own and led her here.

Just *why* she had come was equally nebulous.

All those comments which Miguel had made about her in those private communications—the ones which'd been shared with Njhay and Gofreddo—continued to sting her deeply.

To be quite honest, she wasn't entirely sure just why she allowed those comments to bother her so severely.

Whenever she had worked—*whoever she had worked with*—there had always been poorly concealed criticisms or chat happening behind her back. Perhaps it was something to do with the circumstances; that she had been invited to join Gofreddo Zito's crew only to have her flaws presented for open discussion without her knowledge. Well, without her knowledge until now.

And then there was the fact that she was required to share the rest of her life with these people.

Wasn't she several shades of *crazy* to even consider accepting such an opportunity without first assuring that these people would leap through walls for her? That they accepted her for just who she was . . . that they *loved* and *respected* her for who she was?

Before she had entirely thought the matter through, she was requesting entrance to Miguel's quarters. She expected him to be out or to ignore her. So she was surprised to find that—almost right away—the door slid open. And that Miguel stood in the gap, staring out at her.

She dwelled for a few beats too long on Miguel's exposed, ripped abdomen and chest—he was wearing his overalls rolled down to his waist. And then there was the tattoo which was visible at his neck, and which temptingly trailed its way down his shoulders and back.

She couldn't quite suppress the urge within her to see *that* tattoo again.

And to learn more about Miguel's history.

It took no small amount of effort for her to look past him into the room. She saw that he had a paper book propped up on his desk. She could see that he had been making notes on a screen as he went. She was of half a mind to remind him to take more care about leaving personal communications out in the open; that he shouldn't follow Njhay's model of information security.

"Hi," Miguel said, risking a smile.

Mackenzie stretched out the pause as long as she believed possible.

When she finally did reply, she couldn't keep the sigh out of her voice. "Hello."

What had passed for a smile on Miguel's lips withered and died.

Mackenzie was certain—just for a moment—that he was going to offer an apology. And that she was going to have to think less of him for doing so.

In the end, she was only half right.

"I want to apologise about how you found out," Miguel said. "About how you found out just what I *said*."

Mackenzie held herself still. "You had no duty to tell me what your personal opinions on me were."

Miguel shrugged one shoulder. "I gave those opinions because I was asked for them—and I thought that they would be kept confidential." He shrugged again. "I guess I was wrong. And it was wrong that you had to read those comments in the way you did."

Mackenzie allowed the silence to spread out between the two of them. She was waiting for him to do that cowardly *manly* thing and simply break down—*beg* her for forgiveness.

But he held off.

He held his counsel.

Only his warm, beautiful eyes fixed on hers.

Feeling as if she had made him suffer enough, Mackenzie glanced about the hallway, then said, "Can I come in?"

Miguel had the tenacity to consider this request.

Finally, though, he cracked a smile.

"Sure," he replied. "Come on in."

Mackenzie wasn't quite certain just how it happened. The best way she could think to describe it to herself later on was that she *fell* into him. It was instinct. Something which struck her so strongly that it seemed an urge almost impossible to resist.

Perhaps it was the power of naked, well-worked muscles.

Maybe it was *those* warm eyes.

Or the woody scent which seemed to cling to his skin.

Mackenzie now understood what people meant when they described another as 'irresistible'.

The two of them grinned widely as they tumbled over one another.

Once Mackenzie had taken care of Miguel's clothes—once she had left them in a pile at their feet—she really got to work.

First of all she shoved the book which lay propped on the desk to the floor.

It fell with a satisfying *flutter* of pages.

Its spine splayed and facing up at them.

She ran her fingers through his buzz-cut hair, feeling the perfect form of his skull underneath. She allowed her fingertips to trail down the back of his neck, feeling all of the ripped muscles, and the frantic throb of his heartbeat.

Then she drew him up to her.

She *tasted* him.

Together they set a frantic rhythm.

Both of them hungry to go *faster* . . . but Mackenzie seemingly more so.

Seemingly *hungrier*.

She felt her whole body heat up and then cool down.

She got the idea into her head that there might be an issue with the ventilation systems—that they might be blowing alternatively hot and cold air . . . but she soon realised that it was her own body; that she herself was responsible for the dramatic changes.

As they collapsed together, down onto the bed, Mackenzie allowed Miguel to relax for no more than a minute before leading him by the hand to the bathroom.

The two of them could do with a shower after all that *frantic* activity.

Just to give them a shock, she turned the cold tap up full.

Then she grabbed hold of his flanks, forcing him up against her.

Their eyes met.

Fixed together.

And then, just as she prepared to kiss him, she said, "What do you think blasting off into space does to your sex life?"

Miguel held off for another moment or two.

Then he broke into a smile.

"Well," he said, lowering his mouth to her earlobe so that his warm breath brushed against her neck, "I suppose that depends on the person."

29

LUNAR COMPLICATIONS

*W*hen *Mackenzie had been summoned* to attend a meeting in the secret basement of the Shuttle Hangar, she had been caught in two minds.

On one hand, she had made up her mind—or *thought* she had—that it would be nothing but reckless for her to go off into space; for her to leave the Earth behind forever. It was just like Diane Drake had said:

You still have so much to give—here on Earth.

But did she really?

Mackenzie supposed that it was this doubt which led her to going along to the meeting as planned. Even as she settled down on the landing pad outside the Shuttle Hangar, however, she couldn't say for certain what she was going to say; how she was going to announce her intention. She couldn't help but feel that

Gofreddo had announced the meeting so that they might go public with the plans for the launch.

He wanted a straight yes or no.

As was her habit, Mackenzie was the first to arrive.

There were a few Shuttle pilots hanging about the Hangar but she managed to negotiate them without too much difficulty.

In truth, they seemed more wary of her than she was of them. They no doubt were put on edge to see that the Supervisor of Human Resources was on the prowl in *their* patch of the woods . . .

She located the manhole concealed in the locker room without any aid—and ensuring that none of the pilots caught sight of what she was doing. How much the pilots actually knew about Gofreddo's plan, Mackenzie had no idea. She supposed that there was such a thing as pilot-to-pilot confidentiality . . . something like an omertà.

Perhaps it was from one of the pilots that the leak Kyra Singh had mentioned had come about?

She descended the ladder. She felt strangely weightless as she burrowed deeper and deeper into the darkness. It draped over her like a damp blanket. Her heart beat up in her throat. Despite herself—despite being into her *thirties*—she still held a fear of the dark.

If she'd been really serious about defeating this stupid hang-up then she might've thrown a few thousand at a therapist. Until now it hadn't occurred to her that it was a reasonable business expense.

When she hit the ground, the lights blinked on automatically, apparently sensing her motion. The ship itself stood up on its raised platform—like an actor standing in the spotlight of an empty stage; in a vacated theatre. There was something mournful about the sight, about the rather ugly-looking craft. She couldn't quite shake the feeling that such a vehicle would never fly at all.

The others arrived about five minutes later, and Mackenzie was glad that they did.

While she'd been waiting, she'd taken the opportunity to clamber up beside the spaceship and to peer in through the windows. To get a good look at the interior. Of what would be her home for the remainder of her life . . . unless they found some sort of a habitable, Earthlike environment, of course.

Gofreddo Zito was the last to arrive.

Mackenzie couldn't help but feel the cynical thought sneaking into her mind that he had planned things this way. That he had wanted to be the one that everyone else waited for. That he had the chance to make a Grand Entrance. Well, he had succeeded in any event.

Mackenzie looked to Louise and Njhay—Njhay with his arm about her shoulders.

Both of them had that newlywed glow.

Mackenzie couldn't help but feel somewhat pleased with herself. She was the one who had been ultimately responsible for their wedding. If something had gone wrong then it would've been on her, but because it had gone so perfectly it only followed that she was responsible for that success too.

She looked to Alicia, beside Gofreddo, the two of them chatting in low tones.

And Mackenzie couldn't help but take note of the loving expression smeared across each one of their faces.

She shifted over onto Lan and Patrick.

Patrick stood behind Lan, his arms locked about her neck as if he padlocked the two of them together. *Forever.*

Next, Mackenzie took in Kyra and Julius.

Kyra leaned her head up against Julius's neck, and he was combing his hands through her sleek, beautifully smooth hair.

Finally, Mackenzie found her stare inevitably falling onto Miguel.

It was almost as if he had scanned the state of her thoughts—almost as if he had been tracing the direction of her gaze. As if the same imaginings had been passing through his head. She and Miguel were surrounded by couples. Almost as if the evidence of their inevitable destiny stood around them.

Miguel took a few steps toward Mackenzie.

She felt his fingers brush her hand.

She made no motion to take his hand.

And he didn't go any further to taking hers.

They just stood beside one another.

It was then that Gofreddo Zito began to speak.

He addressed the room as he always did, with a bright, wide smile, and an expression which betrayed the belief that he *owned* the audience; that this audience were some sort of evangelical followers. And, in a way, Mackenzie supposed that he was right.

The way that Gofreddo stood up straight—how he arched his back—Mackenzie couldn't help but wonder if he had studied great leaders throughout history; hoping that he might be able to pick up some tips. But, then again, she supposed that he had had the opportunity to study one of history's great leaders up close:

His own father, Costantino Zito.

"Thank you for coming at such short notice!" Gofreddo said, his voice booming, occupying the entirety of the basement. "I wish to make it clear that you know—before I make the announcement —that each and every one of you here is important." He bowed his gaze dramatically, shaking his head. "No, no, no," he continued, "You are not merely *important*—you are *indispensable*."

Despite herself—despite being well-acquainted with all manner of corporate speech—she couldn't help the tingle which passed through her veins. The sensation twitched through her chest and up to her heart, making it throb several times. When Gofreddo swept the room with his gaze, she was all too aware of him fixing his attention directly on her.

"This mission," Gofreddo said, thrusting a finger up in the air as he resumed, "it is nothing but the realisation of lifetimes of work . . . of all those men and women who precede us." He paused a moment. When the light caught his eye, Mackenzie was certain that she saw a tear twinkling there. "Of my *grandfather's* lifetime." He drew breath, again arching his shoulders back and appearing to grow several centimetres in stature. "For so long mankind has been distracted. Down on Earth . . . playing in the sandbox." He pointed upward, to the basement roof. "Now, though, it is our chance to explore the universe. To see what is *really* out there. To *know* the universe's deepest secrets."

Mackenzie couldn't help but feel inspired by these ideas being thrown around.

When she took in the reaction of the couples, she saw that they were equally swept up by the romanticism of Gofreddo's ideas—not to mention the passion which he utilised to convey them.

She turned back to Gofreddo again.

"Friends," he continued, "the time is nearly upon us—it is nearly the time for us to let the world know about our ambitions. For the world to know what we are *planning*." He broke into a wider grin. "And not only that . . . but to show them that it is *possible*."

Mackenzie felt as if Gofreddo was moving closer toward empty sentiment now—not that she was about to interrupt him. This wasn't *her* mission after all . . . she was only potentially sacrificing what remained of her life for its sake . . .

"It is with great pleasure that I am able to announce that we shall make our plans public next week—on Monday."

Mackenzie felt her chest tighten.

Although she had anticipated that this was the motive for calling the meeting, it felt somewhat devastating that it was being set in stone.

It was then that the focus of Gofreddo's gaze shifted. It passed over the heads of his audience. With the others, Mackenzie followed his eyes. Saw who he stared at.

Karolin Köhler.

Frau Köhler.

She gave a curt nod and a smile, acknowledging the room.

"I'm sorry for arriving late," she said.

"Not at all," Gofreddo replied. "In fact, you have arrived just on time."

It appeared that Gofreddo wasn't finished yet.

When Mackenzie turned back to him, she saw that he was smiling very widely indeed.

"The launch itself shall take place at the end of our current rotation."

Mackenzie's whole body was uncomfortably rigid now. She was glad that Miguel wasn't touching her, because if he had been then it would've been easy to read her exact state of mind.

Just how *worried* she truly was.

Because she didn't know what her decision would be.

Would she stay?

Or would she go?

30

TIME-LIMITING FACTORS

*M*iguel *trod his way* down the corridor of the Crescent Gardens laboratories. He had always felt something of an affinity with the laboratories. Another one of those markers—like the Armstrong Archive—which confirmed that Celestial Stays wasn't entirely profit-driven.

Today, though, there were other things on his mind . . . things *other* than merely academic matters.

He made a beeline for Njhay Garcia's office.

When he peered in through the doorway, he saw Njhay was working away busily at a screen. He was tapping and swishing— off in his own world.

For a few seconds, Miguel did nothing but reflect on the sight; that he himself could be found frequently in a similar pose, only with a book, or a pile of documents to leaf through. The two of them shared their quest for knowledge . . . the two of them wanted to learn *more*.

Because Miguel had been interrupted more times than he cared to count—and he had grown particular about the ways in which it was 'acceptable' to interrupt him—he hung back in the doorway, waiting until Njhay broke away from his work long enough to glance about his surroundings.

Njhay smiled upon seeing him.

Almost as if he'd been caught red-handed doing something he shouldn't have been, he backed away from the screens, setting his eyes upon Miguel.

"Anything I can help you with?" Njhay asked.

Miguel held himself still. He wasn't entirely sure why he had decided to come here. He was certain that he had already made his mind up . . . and yet, he couldn't quite shake the romance off the thing—off the proposal. He wanted to be sure.

"You know that I respect you," Miguel said.

Njhay pouted momentarily. "Well, I'm pleased to hear that—I want you to know that I respect *you* too . . . and all you've done in the name of research during your time beneath the Celestial Stays Dome. Even if it doesn't get the recognition it might deserve."

"Yeah," Miguel continued, wincing slightly, already feeling that he was getting side-tracked, "I wanted to ask about the mission. I wanted to know, well, if you've been having any second thoughts. Any . . . *doubts?*"

Even as Miguel heard the words pass his lips, he couldn't help feeling that he had got his phrasing wrong. That he had kicked things off on the wrong foot. And yet once these words had been said it was impossible to take them back.

Njhay, however, appeared thoughtful.

He poked his tongue hard into one of his cheeks.

Then he replied.

"Nope," he said, smiling widely. "I can't say that I have." He looked about the lab as if he was sizing up his domain. "I feel like

I've hit the ceiling of everything I ever wanted to achieve on the Moon." He looked back at Miguel. "Of course I *could* continue here —I *could* get more and more granular, work on more and more projects, but"—he paused momentarily as if working out how best to put his thoughts into words—"I've become a little too *comfortable* here. I always thought that this—the *Moon*—would represent my life's work." He grinned wider still. "Guess I was wrong, though?"

Miguel thought on this for a long time. Of course, it was impossible to deny that Njhay venturing into space would represent for him a rich array of resources such as no scientist in human history had ever had the chance to explore. But there was something about Njhay's enthusiasm which rubbed Miguel up the wrong way . . . something which he couldn't quite put his finger on but which bothered him immensely. Finally, Miguel settled on what he identified to be the issue. "You're not bothered about *never* returning to Earth—about *never* going back there?"

Njhay pouted then gave a shrug. "To do what?" he said. "Whatever I turned out doing I'd still be in a lab; locked away inside somewhere, working hard. The way I see it, it doesn't seem to make much difference just where that lab happens to be . . . it'd be the same routine for me." Here the corners of his mouth turned back in a smile. "Just the life choices I've made, I guess." He drew breath, as if having just stumbled across another factor. "Gofreddo's got a VR unit installed on the ship, too—so it's not like we can't 'go back' to Earth whenever we feel like it . . . it's not like we won't ever feel the breeze or the raindrops or whatever else gets you going nostalgia crazy for Old Blue."

Miguel couldn't help but find the nickname Njhay had already applied to Earth to be equal parts cute and creepy. There was something about this whole idea which just seemed . . . *off* to him .

. . and yet he couldn't shake the idea from his mind. However, whatever the importance—the *weight*—of the issues they might be discussing here, Miguel realised that this was his opportunity to turn things around. To flip the conversation in the direction he'd hoped it would head toward.

"I wanted to ask about . . . Mackenzie," Miguel said.

Njhay blinked several times. His smile faded. It was almost as if Miguel had given Njhay a slap on the side of the head and he was reeling from the impact.

" 'Mackenzie' ?" Njhay repeated back to him.

Miguel nodded. "You know, that discussion we had with Gofreddo—about whether or not she would be a valuable crewmember . . . about whether or not she would be a suitable person to take along with us on the voyage."

Njhay considered this a long time.

Finally, he regained that previous, easy smile.

"I hope you'll accept my apologies," Njhay said. "When I made those comments—when I solicited your commentary—I did so with the understanding that there was . . . *uh* . . . nothing . . . *going on* between the two of you, I—"

Miguel waved away these concerns. "Don't worry about that," Miguel said. "No hard feelings. Nothing like that. I just want to know what you concluded . . . what swung you around . . . clearly you're happy to head off on the voyage *even if* Mackenzie will be on board?"

Njhay breathed in deeply then sighed long and hard. "My concerns were rooted in the understanding that this would primarily be a *scientific* mission."

Even despite the now-serious tone of the conversation, Miguel and Njhay couldn't help but exchange a pair of wry grins.

Njhay continued, "However, after speaking at length with

Gofreddo, I was able to understand his reasoning for his crew selection. That it will take *all* sorts to keep the ship flying. To complete the mission." Apparently sensing that Miguel wanted more by way of explanation, Njhay went on, "The argument which I brought up with Gofreddo had to do with the fact that we didn't have many people that *needed* managing . . . that we didn't *need* someone to tell everyone to do." He shrugged. "To tell the truth, that was one of the factors which most attracted me to the mission in the first place. *Unchecked* scientific progress, eh?"

Miguel nodded along, understanding where Njhay was coming from.

"It just . . ." Njhay continued, "felt as if it was going to be a disappointment." He shrugged again. "But I came around in the end. Everywhere—and in all circumstances—sacrifices have to be made."

Miguel allowed these noble words to float about the lab. He couldn't help but think how the Earth would be losing what might well have potentially been one of its greatest minds.

Could he say the same about himself . . . *without* sounding like some egomaniac?

Njhay slipped a glance over to his screen, clearly wanting to return to work as soon as possible. Miguel was certain that he was getting in the way of some vital piece of research or other. It was only when he was in the company of someone who was at least as studious as he was himself that he realised just how others might feel—how they might feel that they were wasting time which might otherwise be far more valuably allocated.

"Just one more thing," Miguel said, although it pained him to keep Njhay from returning to work.

Njhay pressed on a smile. Miguel supposed that—like him— Njhay had an introverted tic which tripped him into a sort of neutral *polite* reaction to any real-world intrusions which impressed themselves on him. And, like Miguel, he no doubt wanted to deal with the interruption as efficiently and as frictionlessly as possible.

"When Gofreddo selected the crew, did he expect that Mackenzie and I would get together? That the two of us would end up being a *couple* like the others?"

Njhay blushed slightly.

Miguel was certain that this wasn't the sort of Man Talk which was normally acceptable. But, then again, he hadn't ever paid that much attention to social niceties; in either their male or female forms. He didn't really know quite what *was* acceptable.

"I . . . heard some rumours," Njhay replied. "There were some, uh . . . *mutterings.*"

It was as Miguel had anticipated, not that he was at all put out or angry—not even *ruffled*—by the revelation. He merely gave a nod, and then looked Njhay in the eye and said, with a smile, "I guess Frau Köhler will be the only one flying solo."

Clearly pleased to be allowed to return to his work, Njhay gave a smile in reply, then said, "I suppose so."

Once Miguel had turned his back on Njhay—and the Crescent Gardens lab—the smile quickly slipped off his lips. He had hoped that he would be able to reach some conclusion on whether or not he would take up the offer.

And he still felt as lost as ever . . .

31

MEDIA BRIEFING

hroughout the coming days, it was almost impossible to turn a corner, or catch a PEAR, without hearing something of what Gofreddo Zito had planned; that he had decided to take his sizeable inheritance and use it to fuel his mission to the stars.

Everyone had an opinion on the project, of course, and Mackenzie was most certainly among them . . . in fact, she supposed that since she was entwined in the entire proposal she had a much stronger opinion than most.

Mackenzie glanced up from her desk in the Lunar Grand, seeing the doors to the lift sliding open.

It was Kyra Singh standing there.

She had a couple of journalists hanging back sheepishly on her heels. Mackenzie consulted her agenda and recalled that she had agreed to an interview; and that this was merely what she had arranged coming to pass. The announcement was scheduled to take place tomorrow.

Lunar Landings would release the information.

And the rest would be history.

Because Mackenzie—or Miguel, for that matter—hadn't come down on either side of the joining or not joining of Gofreddo's crew, it was assumed that Mackenzie would be going until such a time that she confirmed that she would not.

The ball was very much still in her court.

Mackenzie looked to Charlie, who sat in one of the chairs standing up against the wall of the office, and flirted with the idea of dismissing her. There seemed to be little point. She would only hear about all this soon enough, and it wasn't like Zito's Quest to the Stars—yes, that name really had stuck—was the best-held secret.

Actually, seeing that Charlie would be taking on Mackenzie's role in short order it would only be of benefit to Celestial Stays if she was kept informed of all the latest developments. And Mackenzie also valued the psychological boost it would no doubt grant Charlie to see that she was being trusted with such 'confidential' information. To be quite honest, confidence was probably the weakest of Charlie's attributes, and the one which she could most do with having bucked up and boosted.

Mackenzie smiled and nodded Kyra into the office, the two journalists following.

Kyra took her seat in one of the chairs while the journalists hung back by the door, looking on.

Mackenzie couldn't help but imagine the two of them acting as some sort of security detail. She banished such thoughts from her mind. She was free to leave whenever she wanted. She was free to tell Kyra to *do* whatever she wished.

"How're you holding up?" Kyra asked.

"How're *you* holding up?" Mackenzie replied, with a slight

smile. "I'm not the only one who's going to be leaving the Earth behind forever in about a month's time."

It was instinct, more than anything, that led to Mackenzie studying the pair of journalists accompanying Kyra. She supposed that she was searching for any sign of surprise; any sense that they were on the cusp of a *scoop* . . . but the journalists took this information in their stride and Mackenzie decided that they already knew all the ins and outs of what was coming next; that would only have made sense seeing that *Lunar Landings* would be reporting on the launch itself.

The journalists *needed* to be prepared.

And then there was the interview which was about to take place.

Mackenzie didn't imagine how it would be possible for Kyra to ask all the questions she would want to ask without those accompanying her knowing the full score.

Kyra gave a shrug. "I feel like I'm already there—on the ship —you know?"

Mackenzie didn't really know. In fact, she had a *really* tough time even *imagining* what it would be like once she was up there, and in the ship . . . assuming that she accepted being counted among the crew, of course. There was still time for her to back out; if that was what she *really* wanted . . .

Kyra turned her gaze out through the window, and onto the lunar plains. "I can't *wait* until we're there." She looked back at Mackenzie. "It will be the greatest challenge of my life—of *all* our lives, I should imagine."

As Mackenzie listened to Kyra's response, she couldn't help but feel Charlie's eyes upon her. She could tell that Charlie knew what she was thinking. You didn't follow someone around for as long as

Charlie had without learning to see the patterns which gave away their thought processes.

Charlie would *know* that Mackenzie was unsure.

The questions began, searching out details of Mackenzie's history—of the life she had led back down on Earth. Kyra seemed keen to make much of Mackenzie's business dealings, especially wanting to pin down the quantity of money which Mackenzie had earned doing what she did. Although Mackenzie didn't push Kyra too hard on her agenda, she could tell that Kyra's job would be to sell the crew to people back Earthside; to *sell* these people who had agreed to jet off into Outer Space as somehow exceptional individuals.

Heroes, even.

Mackenzie wasn't certain she was comfortable with being labelled as a 'hero' of any sort. To her own mind, every last thing she had done throughout her life had been for her benefit alone. She had wanted to better herself.

When Kyra reached the end of the questions, Mackenzie couldn't help but feel a strange sense of anti-climax dawning over her. It seemed almost as if this might be her final interaction on any sort of meaningful level with the People of Earth. Even though she tried to convince herself that this would not be so, that Kyra would be sending back reports—Ship Logs—frequently, she couldn't quite seem to shake this reading of the situation.

As Kyra rose to leave, Mackenzie had the urge to demand that she stay.

That the two of them *talk things out . . .*

But Mackenzie couldn't find her voice.

She remained in her seat, behind her desk.

And then Kyra—and the two journalists—were gone.

With only the two of them remaining, she shifted her attention onto Charlie.

Charlie, she was surprised to see, was smiling.

"I remember when you told me that to be afraid is to grow—that fear is a symptom for a person who continues to challenge themselves."

Mackenzie drew in a deep breath then looked out over the lunar plains. "Yeah?" she replied. "I say lots of things, don't I?"

Mackenzie wasn't entirely sure what had brought her to the Stellar Tide Cultural Centre. She supposed that it was the same urge which had taken her back to Miguel—which'd led her to turning up at his door and forgiving him making those hurtful comments.

It was simply an impulse.

The sense that she needed to do *something*.

It was only slightly surprising that she bumped into Julius Denisov—the Guardian in charge at the Stellar Tide. As was his wont, he strolled along the corridors, looking in on the various galleries, the cinemas, the other 'cultural' features, and checking that everything was running smoothly. Although Mackenzie wouldn't have believed his transformation if she had been merely *informed* of it, she found it undeniable now that it stared her in the face.

Julius Denisov who had once been just about the most rogue of all the rogue characters beneath the Celestial Stays Dome, and responsible for running the Stellar Tide when it had been a casino.

Now, though, it seemed that his relationship with Kyra Singh—the editor of *Lunar Landings*—had changed him utterly. He was unrecognisable as the man he had once been.

"Help you?" Julius said, casually.

Despite Julius's slick expression, the way that he clutched his hands behind his back, Mackenzie was certain not to take his appearance as any sort of assurance of his current state of mind. She knew that he would be just as riled about what they were all going through—about the *prospect* of what they were all *about* to go through—as any other member of the fledgling team.

"I was just . . . taking a walk," Mackenzie replied.

Julius arched his eyebrows. " 'A walk' ?" Finally, his stern, controlled, outward exterior cracked. He could apparently no longer keep his true emotions hidden. He smiled wryly. "Some people take 'a walk' but not Mackenzie Angliss." He gave her a playful nudge on the upper arm. "You must have *some* goal in mind?"

Mackenzie was on the brink of telling him that this wasn't the case when she realised—*frustratingly*—that he had been right all along. The reason she had decided to take a walk was because she'd wanted to clear her mind, or, more precisely, confide in *someone* . . . and, well, if there was anything at all which could be said for Julius he *was* someone.

Deciding that she needed to regain the upper-hand somehow, Mackenzie decided on a plan of action. "I was just speaking with Kyra."

She studied Julius's features.

And was pleased to see that he looked surprised—taken off guard.

It meant *her* advantage.

Mackenzie continued, "Telling her everything there is to know about me for the announcement tomorrow." She cocked her head to one side. "Did she already interview you?"

Julius looked uncomfortable for a couple of moments before he rediscovered his composure. "Yes," he replied, matter-of-factly. "We got it done last night." He broke into a wicked smile. "In *bed*."

Mackenzie hoped that the somewhat sleazy nature which Julius presented was only a façade; that it wasn't how he *truly* was when he was alone with Kyra. Because if that was how he truly was with Kyra then Mackenzie could feel only pity for the girl. Then again she *was* a Big Girl . . . and Big Girls should be able to make up their minds on their own . . .

"Any second thoughts?" Mackenzie asked, then focussed on him.

In her years of dealing with people, she had learned that there was a great amount she could garner about them from their reactions rather than their actual words.

Indeed, she had always believed that people placed *far* too much stock in mere words when there were whole *oceans* of unspoken communication there for the reading.

Frustratingly, though—perhaps what made him such a competent poker player—Julius maintained a straight face as he replied, "None at all. What about you?"

Mackenzie gave the notion of laying it all out for Julius a moment's thought, but then discarded the idea. She was best off speaking with someone else . . . if she decided to speak with someone else *at all* . . . However, before she left Julius behind, she couldn't help one final parting query.

She knew—at the very least—that Julius would give her an honest answer.

He put on no pretension that he *liked* her . . .

"Do you really think I'd be valuable?" Mackenzie asked. "I mean, do you think that I'd be *useful* to the mission itself? That I wouldn't just get in the way—piss everyone off?"

Julius held her eye with a lingering glare. And then, right when it seemed that he might make some excuse and wander off to see to one of his—no doubt—many duties, he replied.

"Yes," he said.

And then, with a brief smile, he took his leave.

It was only a few seconds after that when Mackenzie had a chance to fully analyse the answer.

And she muttered a silent curse to herself that she hadn't taken the opportunity to fight back.

If she and Julius *were* going to ride on the same ship for the rest of eternity then there was no chance that she would allow him to get all his own way . . .

It seemed inevitable that Mackenzie would return to the Basements.

Although she had toyed with the idea of again turning up on Miguel's doorstep—and, quite frankly, the prospect of hours of wild sex certainly *was* a persuasive angle—she decided to take the more measured, introspective approach and headed for the gym.

Once she'd worked up a sweat on various machines—and she could feel what seemed like every muscle and bone in her body aching—she headed down the many steps to the swimming pool. It was there that she soon found she wouldn't have the pool to herself.

Lan Niu was swimming lengths—*backstroke*—a black, rubber hat tugged down over her long black hair. A pair of goggles turning her almost into an alien creature with pupil-less, bulging eyes.

Mackenzie thought about backing out of the pool—of going back to her apartment for a shower—but she managed to arrest her retreat. She forced herself to take the few steps toward the edge of the pool, and then to crouch down and slip into the water.

There was something heavenly about submerging herself.

Maybe it had something to do with long-forgotten memories of her mother's womb.

For the longest time, Mackenzie just stood slouched in the water, her shoulders just about protruding from the surface. She felt the cool air rushing over her moist skin. She silently observed Lan turning lengths in the pool—the mechanical motion of her arms as she propelled herself through the water with grace.

Mackenzie wished *she* might be such an elegant swimmer. But, then again, it was impossible to be good at everything and swimming—quite frankly—had always seemed to come near the bottom of her list of priorities.

Mackenzie was just considering getting out—and taking a *long* hot shower before going for a nap—when Lan brought a soaking hand down on the edge of the pool with a staccato *slap!*

Mackenzie flinched slightly at the sound, and found herself staring into Lan's eyes, behind the dehumanising goggles.

"Didn't see you come in," Lan said, prising the goggles away from her face, and bringing them to rest on her forehead; just below the rubber cap she wore.

Mackenzie regained her swagger. "I'm sly like that," she said, with a smile.

Lan propped her elbows up on the side of the pool, elevating her body up through the water. She bobbed up, her toes protruding through the surface. "It's going to be strange," she said. "To leave all of this behind—to never return to Earth."

Mackenzie thought on Lan's comment.

She wondered how she might reply.

What could she say to *that* . . . besides the obvious 'yes'?

Thankfully, Lan apparently wasn't in desperate need for Mackenzie to answer her question. She drew in a deep breath—which made her float on the surface of the pool—before breathing it out.

She sank with her exhale.

She glanced to Mackenzie. "Have you made up your mind yet? Have you decided?"

Mackenzie fully understood the implications of how she chose to answer Lan's question. She knew that if she told her, *yes, she would be going*, then it would only serve to commit her in some way . . . even if it was only in her own mind.

Even if it was only to her own subconscious.

And Mackenzie wanted to give her mind peace.

She wanted to make her decision *calmly*.

Anything else might prove to be a disaster.

"Uh-huh," Mackenzie finally replied.

Lan widened her eyes, but she said nothing else.

The two of them just soaked there.

In the *pool*.

It may have been as short as ten minutes, or as long as an hour, but it was Lan who finally lifted herself up and out of the pool, giving a yawn as she went.

Mackenzie observed Lan's perfect figure as she crouched down for a towel then wrapped it about her shoulders. It was an odd prospect to Mackenzie to think that there were many who thought that she was beyond jealousy . . . because of her *own* looks. Although she had heard herself spoken about in terms of her 'beauty'—or however she chose to define it—she had always believed herself to be somewhat gawky, *awkward-looking* . . . certainly not 'pretty' in the traditional sense.

Then again, perhaps she was the worst judge.

Lan paused only briefly to wish Mackenzie a good evening, and to give her a wink, which Mackenzie interpreted as communicating good luck.

Once she was alone, she turned her attention to the ceiling of the pool, and to the many panels which made it up. There she saw uncountable dots—like *stars* in the sky. It was hard to believe that their ship would be anything more than a drop in the ocean.

Was it even possible for them to make the slightest difference?

In the end, it was after Mackenzie had hoiked herself free of the swimming pool—and then into a hot shower—that she stood up on Miguel's doorstep. However, when she asked for permission to enter, a pre-recorded message informed her that he was out . . . that if he was required for any reason then he could be found at the Armstrong Archive.

Mackenzie considered her options.

She thought long and hard about going back to her own apartment.

And going through with the long-fabled nap.

But she resisted the temptation.

This might well be her last night with Miguel.

After tonight they might be going their separate ways.

So she caught a PEAR and ended up at the Armstrong Archive.

She looked in all the usual places for Miguel, but had no luck.

He wasn't in the back room located behind the reception desk.

And neither was he in any of his haunts—in the past few weeks this had constituted the space exploration history sections of the library stacks.

She was on the point of giving up—of writing him a message

and posting it through the Link—when she finally caught sight of him.

Just as she might've imagined, he was sitting at a table, brow furrowed, glasses sitting on the bridge of his nose as he peered down over a book lying there before him.

Mackenzie was quiet and careful. She had seen the looks on Miguel's face when she had startled him from his studies. There was always a trace—*more than a trace*—of annoyance there. A sense that she was solely responsible for standing in the way of some universe-wide breakthrough being made. Whether or not Miguel himself saw her interruptions this way Mackenzie couldn't say . . . but he certainly made her feel like it.

When he looked up from his book—no doubt sensing that he was being watched—she gave him a smile. And he smiled back at her. She stepped into the room and the two of them knew that there was no need for words. They were both surely going through the same mental gymnastics—both of them attempting to make sense of that which awaited them in the near future . . . that which awaited them in the rest of their lives.

Mackenzie didn't allow Miguel to so much as mutter a sound past his lips. She pressed herself up against him. Stopped him from being able to think of anything else. As if to force the issue, she reached down to his sides and seized hold of his wrists. Clamped them within her vicelike grip. He didn't resist. And Mackenzie didn't look around.

If there was anyone nearby then they'd better run.

Or else they might burn up.

Mackenzie took hold of Miguel's waist, helping his overalls down his legs.

For the longest time, she was rendered stunned by the sight of his tightly packed muscles; of the brute strength which Miguel seemed to possess so naturally.

Would such strength be wasted if he decided to float out into the middle of space?

Then again, they *already* were out in space, albeit closer to Earth than they would be later, or *ever* . . . She savoured his flesh, pressing her lips tightly against his own. Feeling their tongues entwine and explore one another in a seemingly ever-lasting embrace.

Her heart beat harder.

And her blood rushed faster to her brain.

Her surroundings appeared to be humming.

Everything seemed to be humming.

When he laid her down gently, she reached up and ran her hands across his pectoral muscles. She felt the subtlest of reactions to her touch. The gentle exhale he gave as he entered her. As they lay together on the floor of the library.

Mackenzie sank her teeth into her lower lip.

Groaned.

And it seemed as if the two of them melded into a single being.

Into a *whole.*

With this revelation on her mind, Mackenzie heard Miguel's voice in her ear, as he muttered, just loud enough to be heard, "I love you."

32

PHRASING REDUNDANCY

*O*nly *now did Miguel feel the rough rub* of the threadbare library carpet against his bare back. Against the tattoo of the stray dog he had shown Mackenzie; one of the very few people he had *ever* shown the tattoo. His whole body felt at peace—a sensation which he hadn't experienced since the night of Louise and Njhay's wedding. As Mackenzie lay across his chest, she felt impossibly hot. She seemed almost to purr as she gently slept.

Even as Miguel had said it—*I love you*—he hadn't been entirely clear that he had meant it . . . no, that wasn't how he wanted to put it . . . what he *realised* he felt was that he hadn't *expected* such words to tumble out from between his lips.

In actual fact, he hadn't thought that he would say anything at all.

Why had he said anything at all?

For all he knew, the two of them might be parted before too long—within the next month!—and they would never see one another again. Even if the two of them decided to stay behind, either on the Moon, or on the Earth, there was a good chance that they would drift apart.

That they would become strangers before too long.

The two of them were so different—they came from entirely different worlds, different contexts. And yet he couldn't help but feel the percussive pounding of his heart; how his whole body went rigid just at the thought of Mackenzie. Of having her to himself for the rest of their lives.

Alone.

Drifting out into space.

Even as Miguel felt these considerations entering his brain, he scolded himself . . . he certainly wasn't thinking with his *brain!*

Mackenzie stirred in his arms. He felt her give a slight exhale. He looked down and realised that her eyes were open. And that she was staring at him.

"Are you ready for what's to come?" she asked.

Miguel thought about this for a moment.

He knew that Mackenzie was talking about the announcement of Zito's Quest to the Stars. But she wasn't asking him *what* he had decided, only whether or not he *had* decided.

He spent a long few moments staring down at her—at the fine red hair which pooled up against his skin. He felt as if his heart might throb clean out of his chest.

Finally, he replied, "Yes, I'm ready."

Mackenzie's beautiful green eyes sparkled with his response, and then, lowering her head into his chest once more, he heard her reply, "Me too."

33

PRESS CONFERENCE ACTIVATION

hen Mackenzie had got herself showered and dressed in a clean pair of overalls it was almost time for her to be at the *Lunar Landings* newsroom—almost time for her to attend the press conference. She had tried her best not to hurry through her routine. Whenever she did that she ended up becoming flustered . . . making mistakes. But it was hard. Especially with decisions of such magnitude no longer on the horizon but right up close.

Despite telling herself over and over that she would arrive late to the press conference, she arrived—*predictably*—ahead of everyone save Kyra Singh, who, as she soon told Mackenzie, had been present at the newsroom since about dawn. She had been lining up all the connections, making sure she had all the Earthside outlets she wished to inform ready to receive the news which they had to impart. Although *Lunar Landings* was a media outlet of its own standing, the media would no doubt have a multitude of questions for the crewmembers—and especially Gofreddo Zito.

Even Mackenzie, who made a point of steering clear as well as she possibly could of gossip rags, knew that Gofreddo had been out of the limelight for quite a while now; and the media outlets were *starving* for a new story surrounding him.

Well, today they would get their wish.

And more.

Kyra indicated one of the several chairs positioned in the *Lunar Landings* newsroom and Mackenzie diligently took her seat there.

When she sat down, she felt strangely calm, as if now that she had made the decision. As if *now* that she had decided that she *would* go along on the voyage she could settle down and forget about solving problems or considering details.

Her mind was eerily quiet compared to how it had once been.

Although neither she or Miguel had said as much—there was really no point for words—it was acknowledged that they would show one another what they had decided by simply turning up, or not, to the press conference today.

Mackenzie glanced across the assorted chairs, seeing that each one carried a nametag attached to it. Despite herself—despite telling herself that it didn't *matter* whether or not Miguel turned up today—she couldn't help but linger a little longer than normal over the seat which was assigned to him. While it was true to say that her mind had become unoccupied in many ways it was equally true to admit that she had shifted her focus—more deeply —onto Miguel.

She couldn't help it.

And she began to wonder what might happen if he *didn't* show up.

One by one or—more exactly—two by two, the couples arrived to the press conference.

First to arrive were Louise and Njhay . . . the Happy Couple . . .

the Newlyweds . . . and whatever other clichés Mackenzie cared to dole out to herself.

As Kyra worked away hard at a screen between them, it felt as if it was somehow forbidden for them to speak; as if to do so would be to disrupt Kyra in her workplace.

Mackenzie only exchanged a silent wave with Louise and a gentle, professional smile with Njhay.

Next up were Lan and Patrick. And, once again, neither one of them said anything.

Like Louise, Lan and Patrick waved to Mackenzie and then took their seats, as if they were worried about disturbing some natural balance to the room.

It was Julius who entered afterward. He paused only briefly to give Kyra a peck on the cheek before she flapped him away, and he resigned himself to also taking a seat along the row of chairs. He grinned to himself—and to Mackenzie—as if he was a naughty schoolboy.

Mackenzie couldn't help thinking that Kyra truly had her work cut out for her if she chose to persevere with Julius . . .

Finally Alicia and Gofreddo entered the *Lunar Landings* newsroom.

While Mackenzie noted the dark rings beneath Alicia's eyes, she couldn't help thinking that Gofreddo looked as if he had never slept better in all his life. He grinned from ear to car and there was a sparkle to his eyes. He grinned and waved at Mackenzie, and Mackenzie felt somewhat sheepish smiling back at him and waving. She couldn't help noticing that Alicia—and then Gofreddo, once she had alerted him—both glanced at the vacant seat which awaited Miguel.

The two of them exchanged a goggle-eyed glance which— Mackenzie supposed—she wasn't meant to see. But she had seen it.

What was that look about?

Was it pity?

Was it a sense of disappointment?

. . . What *would* it mean if Mackenzie jetted off to the stars with this bunch of loved-up couples?

Wouldn't she feel as if she was some eternal third wheel?

As if she was a celestial Old Maid?

. . . And she couldn't help wondering whether—if they did succeed in establishing an off-Earth colony—she might become some sort of apocryphal tale.

And yet . . . she could feel the tug of adventure.

The same one which had led to her accepting the position within Gofreddo's crew by simply choosing to turn up today. Would Miguel really leave her stranded?

As if she sensed the tension taut in the air, Kyra glanced up from the work she was doing on the screen. She looked over the couples, and, very pointedly, to the chair which was unoccupied.

The chair which was to belong to Miguel.

On instinct, Kyra glanced up at Mackenzie, and Mackenzie was certain to meet her stare and to glare her down. If Mackenzie was anything at all—*anything at all!*—then it was resilient. Once she had settled her mind on wanting something then she set about doing her damndest to get it.

And—*dammit*—she certainly wanted this now!

All eyes were on Kyra.

Every one of them sitting in the chairs knew that she was nothing if not a stickler for punctuality.

She had told them that they would commence the broadcast at ten a.m.—Lunar Time—on the dot. And, by the clock which hung off the wall, there couldn't be more than thirty seconds to go.

It was right then that Mackenzie realised she could hear footsteps.

She turned in the direction of the doorway.

Looked there.

However it wasn't Miguel who strode through the gap.

It was Frau Köhler.

Despite herself, Mackenzie formed fists down at her side. She gritted her teeth. She felt angry—*betrayed* . . . and yet she couldn't bring herself to reason why she felt that way.

After all, she had asked nothing from Miguel.

Actually, *he* had been the one who had uttered those words; those simple, solid, yet *powerful* words . . . the words which felt as if they strangled Mackenzie right now.

Mackenzie held her gaze downward. She stared at her boots. She had no urge to look up at the others. To see what *their* reaction to Miguel's absence might be. This was her own situation to suffer through. And she had suffered through worse. She had suffered through both her parents' deaths, and then she had built a life for herself—*all on her own.*

She could do so again.

She could make herself *great* again.

She *would* go down in human history.

When she looked up again, she realised that Kyra—and the others—were staring directly at her.

As soon as they saw her looking, however, they turned their attention away.

They *feigned* that they didn't understand what was going on . . . and yet it was impossible that they *couldn't* know what was going on here.

All of a sudden, she had the urge to get to her feet, to storm out of the press conference, but she soon realised that Kyra had uttered the order for the door to the *Lunar Landings* newsroom to slide shut. It was almost as if she was feeling herself being sealed in a personal tomb; left to rot for the remainder of her life.

Wasn't that what it would be like on Zito's ship?

She began to feel a twitching sensation down in her toes.

Her heart hammered against her ribcage.

Right when she felt as if she could no longer bear the suspense, she realised she could hear the sound of footsteps outside the newsroom.

She turned her attention to the doorway—*everybody* was looking at the doorway.

They were past the time for transmitting the news down to Earth now.

Mackenzie was certain that many of the Earthside media outlets tuned into the private channel would be checking their connection ensuring that they hadn't somehow been cut off.

When she looked up again she saw him walk through the doorway.

Miguel.

Her partner . . . *for life?*

The press conference went like just about any press conference which Mackenzie had ever been a part of . . . on the Moon, or down Earthside.

As she had predicted—at least to herself—most of the questions surrounded Gofreddo Zito, asking after his plans for this mission, and whether he was qualified.

She had to admit that she was impressed at Zito's handling of each question; how he would bat away the underhand insults about his moneyed background while modestly playing down the honey-coated praise which was just as often thrown his way.

There were questions about Gofreddo and Alicia and whether the two of them might become the second couple to get married on the Moon.

Gofreddo and Alicia—unable to be seen by those media outlets Earthside—exchanged a glance between the two of them.

Just what it might mean exactly, Mackenzie wouldn't have liked to so much as guess.

Since there was no video link it wasn't announced until a good way through the press conference that Frau Köhler herself would be taking part in the journey.

This—predictably—formed the basis of a fresh tide of questions.

And it was welcoming that it removed the focus from Mackenzie, or any other member of the crew who *wasn't* Karolin Köhler or Gofreddo Zito.

As Mackenzie sat watching the rest of the press conference wind down, she couldn't help wondering if Frau Köhler hadn't planned this from the start; as if her entire involvement with the journey—with Zito's Quest to the Stars—hadn't been so that she might make herself a lightning rod for the media scrutiny to come.

As Mackenzie filed out with the others following the press conference, she couldn't help catching Miguel's eye. He gave her the subtlest of smiles . . . but it was enough for her to *know* that he understood the implications of what he had done . . . of what he had done in leaving her waiting, and what it had meant to her when he had finally turned up.

Almost like a reversal of a marriage ceremony in itself.

While it was traditionally the groom who was kept waiting, in this case it had been the bride. And Mackenzie couldn't help wondering if all the wedding business with Louise and Njhay hadn't gone right to her head. Perhaps she had been driven *crazy* by it . . . if only in small ways.

Once they got free of the press conference, it was Gofreddo Zito who spoke to them all.

"Well," he said, in that typically forthright manner of his, "that was the tricky part—it's all downhill from here on out."

Although everyone laughed along and smiled at his quip, Mackenzie couldn't help wondering if most of the laughter wasn't borne out of ill-disguised nerves.

She knew—*herself*—that she was scared stiff.

34

PROGRAMME SHIFT

he next few weeks passed by very quickly indeed.
At times, Mackenzie wasn't completely sure that she was conscious.

Everything which was happening around her seemed to be playing out in some giddy and distant dream. Her days were thoroughly occupied. She spent a good portion of the day working with Charlie, going through all of the tasks which the Supervisor of Human Resources would be responsible for. As she went about her work, Mackenzie was aware of Frau Köhler more than once skirting her footsteps. It was somewhat unnerving, and, wondering what Frau Köhler was up to, she decided to confront her one day.

"Are you certain the girl is up to the task?" Frau Köhler asked, in her typically direct, yet somehow friendly manner.

Despite Frau Köhler smooth delivery, Mackenzie couldn't help but feel the sting to her remark.

There was the matter of Frau Köhler questioning her judgement—that much was obvious—but then there was the practical consideration to take into account . . . that there was no time for Mackenzie to train up another successor.

It impressed Mackenzie in no small way that Frau Köhler still apparently held the same enthusiasm she had always possessed toward the Celestial Stays Dome; she still yearned to see the venture succeed . . . then again, Mackenzie did suppose that the Celestial Stays Dome would be Frau Köhler's legacy. And why *wouldn't* she care about her legacy?

Finally, Mackenzie agreed, with Frau Köhler, that they would settle on a more qualified candidate for the 'interim period'—as Frau Köhler put it—so that Charlie might have the opportunity to build up some more experience in a less-demanding role before taking on the sizeable challenge of becoming Supervisor of the Human Resources Division.

Charlie, too, seemed relieved, and Mackenzie was surprised to note that she wasn't in the least bit 'put out' that someone had gone above her head and removed her from the firing line.

With this aspect of the Celestial Stays Dome administration taken care of, Mackenzie allowed herself to relax somewhat . . . if by 'relax' she had in mind obsessively inspecting each and every nook and cranny of the ship; the Sbrupta Six —now dubbed simply, *ZITO*.

Mackenzie had to admit that the ship itself was decidedly spacious.

There was a living area, complete with a kitchen and several view screens.

As she had heard Njhay mention once, there were also VR units installed so that they could have more immersive experiences when they wished for them. They could 'revisit' Earth at will.

At least within the realms of their minds.

There was a gym—with a swimming pool!—and there was also a sauna and a steam room.

If she had had the opportunity to choose her own prison then *ZITO* would certainly be it.

The personal quarters were also large and accommodating.

Each living space featured a sitting room with a bedroom off through a doorway. There was a deluxe ensuite bathroom in each one of the living quarters too, of course.

Mackenzie could see herself getting very comfortable here.

Perhaps *too* comfortable . . .

Throughout the weeks leading up to the launch, each crewmember was given some non-optional sessions with a psychiatrist.

In Mackenzie's sessions, at least, she was given various techniques which were designed to help her cope with living with a group of people until the end of her life.

Once they had set off with the mission, they would each continue to have therapy on a once-a-week basis which could be increased according to the will of the specific crewmember.

As for Mackenzie, she couldn't see herself going much beyond the once-a-week sessions. But, then again, who was to say how she would feel about the thing in ten years' time?

She might well have lost her nut by then . . . they *all* might've lost their nut by then.

When the launch week itself approached, Mackenzie had a hazy feeling about the whole voyage.

She wasn't certain that it was real.

And matters weren't helped when she received another message from Earthside—courtesy, once again, of Diane Drake.

Mackenzie put off reading the message from Diane for as long as she possibly could. It was almost as if—the longer she ignored the message—the longer it would cease to exist.

Her logic seemed flawless when it correlated with her desire for a clear head . . . when it correlated with her desire to *enjoy* the last moments she had with the Earth; albeit at three hundred and eighty thousand kilometres distance. But there would be no putting off the message.

Even though she knew that they would remain in contact with Earth through a fancy, state-of-the-art messaging system which one of Gofreddo's father's business partners had devised, it felt like she had to reply to Diane while she was still close.

While there was still a *prospect* of her being able to return to Earth.

She took a rare quiet moment to herself, sitting down in her office, looking to the lunar plains off in the distance as she allowed the message to be displayed in her mind's eye, via the Link:

Dearest Mackenzie,

I write to you now knowing the choice you have made. I am extremely glad that you have been able to take the time to really think about this decision—to work out what might be best for you. It certainly shall be a real adventure! Ever since the two of us met under those most unspeakable of circumstances, I have considered you an honorary daughter. It befits all that is in my heart to tell you how much I care; how much I wish you well. And you must also realise that, as a daughter, I feel great, real pain at your departure. But I know that this is for a greater cause. Certainly a greater cause than I could ever have imagined for myself.
Although I realise that it might be in vain, I want to offer you the opportunity to return. I want you to know that—as long as I shall

live—you will have a home with me. All you need do is say the word and you are welcome to come back.

It's never too late.

All my love,

Diane

Mackenzie felt the tears running freely down her cheeks. She wiped them away, smearing them into her skin with her palms.

She felt herself trembling all over—the sobs were determined to come out.

They were determined to make themselves felt.

But it was testament to the image which Mackenzie hoped to project to the world that she first glanced through the glass walls of her office, wanting to check that the floor was really clear before she let herself go completely. Before she submitted to her emotions.

When she was finished with her weeping, she turned her attention back onto the message. She read through it another few dozen times. And then—*a dozen times more*—she attempted, and failed, to compose a response.

In the end, she decided she didn't need a reply at all. She could do without it. There had been no lingering thread from Diane. No request for Mackenzie to tell her 'how things were going'.

A clean break.

Just as it would be with the Earth itself.

The day of the launch was more than surreal.

Mackenzie woke up in her apartment in the Basements with no bags to pack other than the few personal effects she had brought up with her from Earth. There was her mother's hairbrush, and her father's notebook—the one in which he had kept a weather diary.

Whenever she felt like she could no longer cope—which had been often while she'd served beneath the Celestial Stays Dome—she would lie down on her side, on her bed, and gently brush her hair with her mother's brush while reading her father's diary entries.

The format of the diary entries was always the same.

There was the time, and date, and location, and then there was a sentence or two to describe the weather conditions that day. Back when the loss of her parents had still been raw, she had used the diary as a tool to help her fall asleep.

It had never failed.

This week, she had found that she needed the diary more and more often.

It was while she was reading through the diary that she got a message from Louise. She thought it would be something perky—something which might help to get her into the mood to leave all that she had ever known behind her forever.

But there was nothing perky about it.

It was Miguel.

He was . . . *'missing'*.

Still reeling from the message which she had received from Diane Drake earlier, Mackenzie struggled to think what this might mean. She wondered if it meant that the launch would be suspended until he could be found. Or if it would be outright cancelled if he was truly lost.

And then she wondered *how* this might've happened.

What might've brought it on.

Miguel, surely, wanted to be alone for a while . . . Mackenzie was alone right now.

Wasn't it *okay* for him to be alone?

She was on the brink of getting up from her workstation and going to see Louise personally, to clear up the situation, when the Link informed her that there was someone at the door.

That there was someone who wanted entry.

It took her only a second to discover that it was Miguel.

As the door slid back, she was on the lookout for signals—for some sign that Miguel had somehow become psychologically unhinged in the past few days.

He seemed normal to her . . . of course he looked a little drowsy, but then again weren't they *all* just a little drowsy at the moment?

It *was* an enormous undertaking which lay ahead of them.

And one which would live with them forever in more ways than one.

Miguel sat on the edge of her bed. He held his head in his hands. He had said nothing since he had walked into the room . . . and she hadn't wanted to presume so much as to force him to speak. She supposed that all the 'people-hacking' skills in the world wouldn't be able to save her now. She simply had to resort to old-fashioned patience—*patience* would do the trick.

Wouldn't it?

She held her breath even though just about everything within her cried out to say *something* . . . to be able to set the conversation flowing; to make it so that the problem was rolling steadily toward a conclusion. Finally Miguel did say something.

Though it was not what Mackenzie had hoped for.

He spoke almost too quietly for her to make out individual words.

But she thought she could just about understand what he said:

No puedo hacer esto.

I can't do this.

Mackenzie's school Spanish—brushed up on the odd business trip or two—was enough to understand. Despite the message she heard loud and clear, Mackenzie didn't presume to insist. She held her distance. It was imperative that she allow Miguel his time and space.

Just as she often wished for her own time and space.

Finally, he removed his hands from his face.

And he looked up at her.

He had tears in his eyes.

His pupils were dilated.

Jaw latched open . . . seemingly beyond tears.

All of those hallmarks of a broken man which Mackenzie had seen more times than she cared to admit—all of the always painful evidence that it was just impossible to cope.

That the ability of rational thought had long ago departed.

Feeling now that she had a chance to make an impact, she reached out and brushed her fingertips across the back of his hand. He flinched slightly at her touch.

"I'm not going to tell you that you *can* do this," she said. "That decision is personal—it depends entirely on you . . . you have to look inside yourself." She drew back, considering Miguel and her effect on him. "But what has made you shift your mind so dramatically? What has *changed*?"

Miguel held himself still—*impossibly so* . . .

She was worried that he might've lost his mind; that he could quite easily have slipped off to some other world. And that she would never be able to recover him.

Slowly, apparently regaining his senses, he lifted himself up off the bed.

He stood over her.

For the longest second, he met her eye.

And she stared back at him.

Her heart swilled in her throat.

It beat against the back of her tongue.

She tasted a vague flavour of blood . . . *bitter* . . . *coppery* . . .

"*Lo siento*," he said. *I am sorry.*

Mackenzie continued to stare at him. "Me too," she replied. "I'm sorry because I have to go. This is something I have to do." She paused. "With or without you."

35

EMOTIONAL RECOIL

As Miguel stalked away from Mackenzie's apartment in the Basements, he had only one thought on his mind. He wanted to be back at the Armstrong Archive. And he wanted to lose himself—once more—in those lines and lines of text. He wanted to feel all those words washing over him like some ethereal sea . . . ebbing in and out of his mind . . . drawing him away from this world with each syllable that echoed within the realms of his skull.

He *could* escape.

He *still* had time.

He *didn't* need to leave the world behind . . .

When he returned to the Archive, he was certain that he would feel some sense of remorse; that he would regret having left Mackenzie under such circumstances; that he would have left her to go about the journey *alone*.

But, quite simply, he felt nothing much at all.

He reasoned with himself that he was being melodramatic, that it wasn't quite the truth that Mackenzie would be alone, even.

Frau Köhler would be going along on the Quest to the Stars, too; she would be able to provide Mackenzie with company with all of those couples surrounding them.

They had each made their decision.

And they would stick by their choice.

Ever since the press conference, and throughout the one-on-one psychiatry sessions, he had felt as if his soul had been in conflict with itself. He had felt an almost physical weight resting across his scalp, as if some phantom might be gently ducking him in a swimming pool; little by little drowning him. It was with this in mind that he had known that he couldn't remain this way . . . that it would tear him apart if he violated his beliefs so terribly. He had *always* been a man of science, and in some ways he supposed that he was a *slave* to science itself.

Quite simply, to possess the passion which he held, he knew that he could do nothing but abide by its rules and implications. He couldn't accept the place on Zito's ship.

Not in his right mind, he couldn't.

Miguel returned to the familiar reception hall of the Armstrong Archive. He made a beeline for the desk, and then the doorway to the back room.

Throughout his life he had always imagined such doorways—in whatever research institute he happened to be haunting at the time —would lead him to other dimensions; to different places and distinct times. It was the power of the written word which provided him with his escape from the real world, and all its trimmings. He knew now what his calling was.

He was not a practical man; he was a *theoretical* one.

Before Miguel plunged once more into the worlds which occupied his mind, he disconnected himself from the Link. He wanted to know no news of the launch. He didn't want to be *part* of it any longer . . . he wanted to be *alone* here . . . alone with nothing but the voice in his head.

Even after having disconnected himself from the Link, he had barely sat down at the desk and pulled out a copy of one of his favourites for comfort-reading—*Lunar Ramblings: A Casual Astronaut's Guide*—when he felt an odd sensation pass through him.

It was akin to a chilling of the blood.

All at once the hairs on the back of his neck stood up.

His muscles went rigid.

He glanced over his shoulder.

Saw someone standing there.

A reflex caused him to suddenly straighten up.

He sent his chair tumbling back.

It clattered against the floor.

He stared into the gloom, bringing the figure out of the shadows.

He soon recognised who it was, of course.

Gofreddo Zito.

The man's image was so familiar—even to a hermit such as Miguel—that he had some trouble reconciling the actual man with all the gossip-rag photographs and video footage.

They had never known one another on anything much more than handshake terms and yet Gofreddo had decided that he knew enough about Miguel to offer him a place on his spaceship.

With a gentle smile—one which seemed to clash with the infernal demons rattling about his head—Gofreddo took a few steps out of the shadow.

"I thought I might find you here," Gofreddo said to him, in their shared language, Spanish.

It was odd for Miguel to hear his native tongue spoken out

loud. He was so used to conversing in English. In fact, often, he caught himself *thinking* in English, too.

That Gofreddo had spoken to him in his native language seemed to lend a dreamlike quality to their encounter—if the encounter wasn't playing out in a dream itself.

"I understand that you're feeling under duress," Gofreddo said.

Miguel finally managed to snap back some semblance of his senses. He reached up for his glasses, but realised that he hadn't had so much as the presence of mind to put them on before starting into his book. "Yes," was all he could say by way of reply.

"It's a difficult time—for all of us," Gofreddo said. "This single day shall define the trajectory of the rest of our lives. Make no mistake, if any one of us feels anything less than one-hundred-per-cent committed to the project then now would be the time to say so."

He paused, as if waiting for Miguel to confirm his lack of commitment.

Miguel strained to reply that he *did* lack commitment, but he found that his throat was impossibly dry. And his neck muscles had become so flimsy as to be rendered useless. He felt as if all the strength had drained from his body.

Gofreddo gave him another flicker of a smile and then trod up to a bookshelf. He looked along the spines of the books with a slight smirk clinging to his lips. When he reached the end of the row, he flipped a glance over his shoulder. "I first believed something was amiss when you failed to submit any of these books of yours for loading onto the ship." He reached out for one of the books.

Like all of the others on the shelf the pages were well-thumbed and the spine had been cracked in several places.

When Gofreddo absentmindedly turned a few pages, a whole

clump fell out of the middle. With a slight blush, and a mouthed apology, Gofreddo stooped to recover the jettisoned pages. He replaced them within the centre of the book, shut the book once more, then replaced it on the shelf.

Wiping the dust from the books on the trouser legs of his overalls, Gofreddo said, "I couldn't help observing that the rest of the Archive is elaborately ordered—but these books, the ones here on this shelf, I cannot understand the logic to their organisation."

Miguel held himself still for a long moment. Then he managed to find the strength to reply. "I keep these books here because they are—for one reason or another—personal favourites." He strained to say something more but his throat again felt too dry to form words.

Gofreddo pouted. "So, you would say that it was an *emotional* decision—not a logical one—to place the books on this shelf? The motive for wanting these books nearby is one which is borne out of your heart?"

Miguel said nothing. He could tell what Gofreddo was doing—what line of logic he was pursuing—but he wasn't going to fall into the trap. He wasn't going to allow Gofreddo to change his mind. There was no way onto the ship for him now.

Mentally, Miguel had checked out.

Made his choice.

Gofreddo glanced over the books again and then nodded. He paced as he spoke, taking in various other little details of Miguel's back room office—occasionally pausing to inspect one of the many piles of papers which were stacked all over the place. "Have you never thought that someone with your knowledge—with *your* intellect—is wasted sitting about in the dark, cooped up in a corner where he barely sees the light of day?"

Gofreddo glanced briefly at Miguel.

He felt a burning sensation down in his gut.

He tried to hide his discomfort but wasn't sure whether or not he was successful.

That was one of the problems with actively removing himself from social situations, he had lost the practice for controlling his emotions.

"You could be a *great* teacher, Miguel," Gofreddo said. "I have no doubts about that. And I believe that you can bring the past to life better than you imagine." He smiled briefly but emphatically. "I have tagged along on more than one of your tours of the Armstrong Archive—I have felt myself carried along by the wave of enthusiasm with which you inject your work . . . it is for this reason that I knew you would be indispensable for the mission."

Miguel blinked himself out of his daze. "When you say 'indispensable' I don't believe you fully fathom its implications."

Even as he muttered the line, he was aware that it sounded not a little condescending. He was certain that—at times—he could be as condescending as anybody.

He wasn't blind to seeing that he carried a certain academic arrogance around within him.

It was his rock. His foundation. His personal *value*.

Without it he was nothing.

Gofreddo, however, seemed unoffended by Miguel's tone. He tilted his head to one side and smiled gently. "How do you mean exactly?"

"I mean," Miguel replied, finding that his voice was much firmer now, "that to be *indispensable* suggests that something will be *unable* to work—that something shall be *unable to function*— without some constituent part."

Gofreddo said nothing by way of reply.

Miguel couldn't help thinking that he was being more than a *little* condescending now.

"And your point is?" Gofreddo asked.

"Well," Miguel continued, keen not to come across as the arse-hole he was surely painting himself to be right now, "that if I refused to go along on the mission then the mission—quite simply —would not take place."

Gofreddo's features froze.

He eyed Miguel for a long few seconds.

Then gave a light-hearted shrug.

He trod toward him, heading out of the back room office.

Miguel was almost certain that Gofreddo was admitting defeat —that, seeing that his objective was futile, he was taking his leave with his ego intact.

However, just as Gofreddo left through the doorway—and perhaps out of Miguel's life forever—he reached out and gripped his shoulder tightly.

In a quiet voice, Gofreddo said, "Why else do you think I came here to try and change your mind?" And, just like that, Gofreddo was gone.

Miguel stood where he had done throughout their conversation for several seconds. He stared into mid-air . . . into the gloom. His mind formed bizarre, unrecognisable shapes. He felt as if his brain was being kneaded between a pair of brisk, invisible hands.

It was only when he returned to his desk—after retrieving his glasses, laying them across the bridge of his nose and turning the page of his book—that he felt a smile beginning to sneak onto his lips. He shook his head. Chuckled to himself.

Gofreddo was good.

He had to give him that.

He was *good*.

36

FLIGHT PREPARATIONS

ackenzie was surprised that the preamble—ahead of *ZITO's* launch—wasn't all that different from the launches in the Shuttles Earthside; the ones which would send passengers up to the Moon.

The only real difference, she supposed, was that they wore a different set of overalls.

Gone were the dirty-grey flight overalls. As were the royal-blue Celestial Stays garb. They didn't even have on the traditional, burgundy overalls which Celestial Stays guests were required to wear for the duration of their visit. Instead, they all wore Earth-green overalls.

When she had pressed Gofreddo for the reasoning behind selecting this particular colour for the overalls of those on board *ZITO*, he had merely mumbled something about 'nostalgia' and 'dreams'. She wondered if the overalls were supposed to represent some sort of a reminder about where they had come from. And where they were going.

To Mackenzie's mind, at least, there seemed little reason for this souvenir.

She would never lose the memories she held of Earth, or of the Moon. There wouldn't be a single day when she wouldn't wake up thinking about Earth . . . *dreaming* of having returned there.

But it was all for a higher calling.

It was all for the sake of a *grander* adventure.

Each and every one of them on the crew was exceptional.

Each and every one—as Gofreddo was fond of repeating—was *irreplaceable*.

And even as Mackenzie looked around the locker room where they had all been zipping their overalls up over their standard clothing, she couldn't help but begin to think that Gofreddo had been correct. There was Louise with her unwavering determination and innate bravery. Then there was Njhay with his cool, scientific ways. Next was Alicia who could cook up a storm at a moment's notice. As for Gofreddo himself . . . well, where was she to start there?

Lan could sort out any dispute—terrestrial or extra-terrestrial alike—in a matter of seconds. Meanwhile Patrick, as Mackenzie was familiar with from personal experience, could fly just about anything that vaguely resembled a spaceship. When she lingered over Kyra, Mackenzie couldn't help admiring her willingness to do anything—*anything at all*—to achieve her dreams . . . she couldn't care less about the rules. And, as it happened, neither did Julius; although her admiration for him was far more grudging.

Finally, there was Frau Köhler who—like Gofreddo Zito—was larger than life. It seemed that, like Gofreddo, Frau Köhler had already acquired semi-mythical status.

Then again, Mackenzie supposed, at least to the minds of Earth children, all of them who were now boarding *ZITO* would take on that same mythical quality.

They were the ones who had sailed away to the stars.

Never to return.

Mackenzie tried her best not to allow Miguel's absence to bother her. What she was about to take part in now was far bigger than any fledgling relationship the two of them might have shared.

She had made her choice and she would stick with it.

Perhaps it was only right that she do this alone—just as it seemed she had done everything else in her life *alone*.

She drew several deep breaths and then turned her attention onto the others.

Each and every one of them was smiling broadly.

All of them except for Gofreddo.

He looked pure business.

This was *his* dream, after all.

The rest of them were mere bit-part players within it.

Although Mackenzie had spent what amounted to hundreds of hours aboard *ZITO* in the previous month, it felt decidedly odd when she boarded this time. It was of course the knowledge that she would not be very easily able to step back off the ship again . . . not without a spacewalk suit . . . or in the unlikely event they encountered an Earthlike planet.

Was this nuts?

Was this really what she wanted to do with the remainder of her life . . . and *alone*?

Whatever her thoughts, she couldn't help but believe that she had already made up her mind.

There was no turning back now.

One thing was for certain, if she turned down the opportunity she would regret it for the rest of her life. Just as she might regret having stepped onto the ship now.

She hung about near the back of the group. She didn't want to be the first onto the bridge. And neither did she wish to be the last. It seemed that Frau Köhler wanted the privilege of being the last crewmember aboard.

As Mackenzie glanced about, taking in the lunar plains, and the Celestial Stays Dome in the distance, she knew that this was what she had to do.

She looked to *ZITO* and followed on Lan Niu's heels—going aboard.

Once on board, she looked back over her shoulder, seeing that Frau Köhler was dithering—taking her time in looking off at the Dome, and then to Earth.

When Frau Köhler turned back to the ship, she wore a wide smile. Her eyes seemed to be sparkling. Mackenzie had always liked to think that she could see the imaginative thoughts flying about like minute silver bubbles beneath the surface of her eyeballs.

It was only when they got onto the bridge itself and they took up their positions that the reality of the situation struck Mackenzie. Until this very moment, she hadn't allowed herself to believe that this was *really* true . . . but she certainly acknowledged its reality now.

As Flight Director, Mackenzie took up her place in one of the chairs located toward the back of the bridge. She immediately found herself overwhelmed by the sheer quantity of screens—and the amount of information—which glared up at her.

She reassured herself that, for the time being, all that she needed to do was sit down in the chair and buckle up. The take-off would be managed by experts back on Luna. They would take care of all the technical details, too, the trajectory and the velocities, all of that information which, in the coming months—*years, decades*—Mackenzie would become familiar with herself.

That had been part of Gofreddo's plan, that they would all learn the duties required of their particular role in bite-sized chunks . . . they would work on a need-to-know basis.

One of the reasons Gofreddo had selected the crew as he had done was due to his belief in their capacity to learn on their feet. And, to tell the truth, Mackenzie had done more than her share of 'learning on her feet' throughout her lifetime. Why should it be any different floating out in space?

Mackenzie glanced about the bridge, seeing that Patrick Fourie had taken up the pilot's chair. He would be the one responsible for guiding their trajectory once they left the Moon behind. He would be the one who would follow the instructions which Gofreddo set as Captain.

It had also been made clear to them during the preparations for the launch that they would all work together on mission plans; that they would ensure that they operated the ship in a democratic manner. Whether or not this unconventional management struc-ture for a spaceship might prove to be a disaster remained to be seen. Mackenzie, after all, was renowned for having 'strong' opinions.

And a 'forceful' personality.

She looked about the rest of the bridge, to where Alicia—the Ship's Cook—and Lan—Master-at-Arms—sat beside one another.

They were holding one another's hands as they watched their men work the controls; Patrick in the pilot's seat, and *Captain* Gofreddo Zito standing over him.

They appeared to be in heated discussion over something or other.

Mackenzie wondered if it fell within the remit of her duty to interfere. If she was supposed to step in and break any stalemates which might result from such arguments. She supposed so . . . but —as she'd learned through her life of management thus far—it always paid to allow the two sides of any fight to tire themselves out before stepping in.

Otherwise it might end up with both of them turning their attention onto *her*.

When she glanced across the bridge to Kyra, she saw that she held her finger to her earpiece—no doubt making a record of all the events currently transpiring on the bridge. She took on the mantle of the Ship's Journal . . . and was also in charge of the communications as they were relayed back to Earth. Beside her sat Julius, apparently in charge of the nebulous area of 'Entertainment' . . . just what this constituted, Mackenzie had never thought to follow up with Gofreddo. She had decided that—once she had accepted the place upon the crew—she needed to place at least an entry-level portion of faith in Captain Zito.

She took in Njhay who was sitting at the other side of the bridge. As he had always appeared back on the Dome, he was apart from everyone else. He seemed to be off in his own little world.

Mackenzie guessed he was probably conducting a thought experiment of some description at the present moment. If she had got one impression from Njhay it was that he wasn't going to waste a single second of this voyage. He was going to use every last moment he had for scientific purposes. That was whenever he wasn't required in his role of Ship's Doctor.

Mackenzie wondered if Louise truly appreciated what she'd got herself into.

Then again Mackenzie had fallen for the similarly bookish Miguel . . .

As she thought about Louise, it took her off guard to observe her plop down in the chair alongside. Louise aimed a bright, wide grin at her.

Mackenzie had almost forgotten that Gofreddo had made Louise First Mate.

Perhaps it was some sort of a backup measure, so that if anything became of Mackenzie—or Gofreddo, for that matter—there would be someone to step into her shoes. Although it was admittedly practical, Mackenzie couldn't help but feel just slightly put out that people were not only considering her demise but making plans for after it had taken place.

Then again, she supposed she shouldn't be *so* down about it . . . the most likely event was that they would all die together, after all.

"They're arguing," Louise said, leaning into Mackenzie.

"I can see *that*," Mackenzie replied. "But what're they arguing *about?*"

Louise gave Mackenzie a purposefully gormless look then shrugged.

Mackenzie looked back at Patrick and Gofreddo.

Patrick—as if he was required to prove some sort of masculine prowess—had risen out of his chair now. He was really going at Gofreddo.

She had to admit that anyone who took on a fight with Gofreddo came off as the loser right from the start. Gofreddo was as unflappable as he was stubborn.

When she glanced to her right she realised that Frau Köhler had settled into the chair on the other side of her. As if they were still living according to the rules of the Celestial Stays Dome, Mackenzie felt a rush of blood to the head. She blushed slightly.

Frau Köhler didn't seem affected by Mackenzie's reaction, she merely smiled back at her.

Mackenzie could see that Frau Köhler was slightly dewy-eyed . . . then again she supposed that in a matter of minutes all of them would be more than *slightly* 'dewy-eyed'.

Deciding that there didn't seem to be an end in sight to the 'discussion' between Patrick and Gofreddo, Mackenzie rose out of her chair and crossed the bridge.

She stood over them, not bothering to so much as utter a word.

The two of them noticed her out of the corner of their eyes— Patrick with a straight-faced expression; Gofreddo with a wry, almost-embarrassed smile.

Mackenzie decided to make her presence a little more forcefully felt.

"What's the trouble here?" she asked.

Gofreddo merely smiled back at her, offering nothing by way of explanation.

Patrick, however, with a profound sigh, turned to her and spoke.

"He wants us to wait a little longer."

"A 'little longer' for what?"

"For Miguel."

All at once, Mackenzie felt her stomach twist. She felt the eerie sense that everyone on the bridge was staring at her. She wanted desperately to disappear . . . one of those public-embarrassment feelings which she'd believed she'd got shot of forever.

Apparently not.

She glanced to the others, to their wandering eyes. She pressed her lips together tightly. She turned her attention to Patrick, then to Gofreddo. It seemed that this would be her first test as Flight Director. But she made no show of it.

"Let's go," she said, turning as she spoke, making her way back to her seat between Louise and Frau Köhler.

It was only when she had settled down in her chair, when she went about securing her chest straps, that she realised she was shaking violently.

But she was certain she'd made the right call.

There was no place for romance.

Not now.

Not ever again.

Not in *her* life.

As Mackenzie sat tight, watching the Moon disappear smoothly but surely in the vidscreen, a tingling sensation ran through her stomach.

There was the evidence, sitting right before her.

There was no denying what she had done now.

And there was no going back.

As Patrick adjusted the trajectory of *ZITO*—as they left the Moon behind for the last time—he brought Earth into view.

Everyone on the bridge turned their attention to the sight.

No one spoke.

There was only the gentle grumble of the ship's systems around them.

Mackenzie only realised she was crying when she felt a patch of the upper thigh of her overalls damp. Instinctively, she reached up and felt for her nose, believing that it might be bleeding. But the moisture was running down her cheeks; and it was formed of tears.

It took her a little longer to realise that she wasn't only weeping for the Earth which she was leaving behind forever—nor for Diane Drake who she would never see again. She realised that she was crying because Miguel was gone. Because she had condemned herself to a life of loneliness.

To the company of those who surrounded her.

She glanced about, unsure quite what to make of her situation.

What might Gofreddo say if she told him she wanted to return?

It would be just as they had discussed . . . just how they had *agreed*.

Even if someone made a *real* fuss about going home there would be no turning back.

It would be understood to be only a temporary *loss* of sanity. As if the only explanation for them wanting to return *could be* insanity. They had all signed the contract; similar to the one which they had signed when they had agreed to work for Celestial Stays.

There *was* no turning back.

As if she was able to read the thoughts as they tumbled—one by one—through her mind, Mackenzie felt Frau Köhler reach out and take hold of her hand.

To begin with it only served to make her feel worse, to send the tears rolling down her cheeks all the faster, but soon there emerged a warming glow in her heart . . . a sense that everything *would* be okay from here on out . . . if only she could show just a little courage now.

Just a *modicum* of the courage she had shown throughout her life.

Was she capable?

Mackenzie believed she was.

Patrick made another adjustment to the controls.

And the Earth slipped from view forever.

Mackenzie had to blink several times, absorbing the blackness of space—mitigated only by pinpricks of stars—and began what would surely be an eternally long process of making peace with her destiny. Of making peace with what she had signed up for.

Realising the chest straps she wore were no longer necessary, she ran her hands about herself.

Her fingers felt clumsy—*ungainly* . . . finally she found the clasp, however.

And she let it loose.

She half expected the entirety of the bridge to turn and observe her as she took her leave—as she rapidly set off into the ship, to one of the nearby toilets.

But nobody seemed to so much as note her exit.

They, too, she supposed, were being crushed by the levity of what faced them.

The days and days.

The years and years.

The rest of their lives.

It was only when she was alone in the toilet—the door closed behind her—that she really let herself loose. She sobbed into her hands. Felt the tears seeping out between the gaps in her fingers.

She kept on crying until it seemed that she had nothing left to cry.

And then she started up all over again.

37

DISTANCING PATHWAYS

*I*t *was a week into the voyage* when Mackenzie truly made peace with her fate. And the evidence came in the most mundane of forms.

It was a simple realisation.

Nothing dramatic—nothing *earthshattering* . . .

It was simply a *recognition*.

She had just woken with the Link, telling her that her turn for duty was coming up. That she would be expected on the bridge in the next half an hour.

As had become her morning routine, she had risen and taken a shower, before diligently slipping on her overalls. It was while she looked herself over in the mirror that she realised she was smiling.

And that her eyes had a lusty sparkle to them—a *sparkle* like the one which seemed always to be present in Frau Köhler's eyes.

And that was when she knew she was okay.

That what she was doing was *right*.

That she had done *herself* justice.

This wasn't about anybody else—what might be right for them or their lives.

She had gone ahead and made something of *herself*.

When she got to the bridge, Louise was on duty, sitting at the captain's controls. She wasn't actually *touching* anything, of course. There was no reason to *touch* anything for a while yet. Gofreddo had already set their route and they would follow it until their arrival . . . unless they strayed into a bunch of space debris, or similar.

Alicia was taking a break from the ship's kitchens to look over the navigational maps and the communications consoles. She was positioned on the other side of the bridge.

They were the only ones there.

The others were all sleeping or relaxing . . . or . . . doing something *else*.

Mackenzie smiled at the two women and then took up her seat in the now-familiar Flight Director's chair.

The chair itself had already begun to mould to her shape . . . or maybe it was because she was steadily becoming accustomed to the position.

To the position of holding de facto *power* over the entire ship . .

.

She had lulled herself into one of those semi-hypnotised states, staring out at the endless stars and the depths of space when Alicia spoke to her.

"Guys?" Alicia said. "You want to take a look at this?"

Mackenzie remained sat in her chair for several moments, still getting her head around where they were going . . . or perhaps she was trying to get to grips with the fact that they had *nowhere* in particular to go . . .

Whatever the case, she lifted herself out of the Flight Director's chair and made her way across the bridge. To where Alicia sat at the communications.

Louise, too, came over.

"It's from Luna," Alicia said.

They had been receiving messages from Luna every day or so. Most of them were standard and uninteresting. Just status reports or well-wishing . . . not that these reports and well-wishes weren't appreciated . . . but they were hardly much more than their functions suggested.

This message, however, was quite different.

Mackenzie read it aloud, "Special delivery?"

Louise and Alicia said nothing.

Apparently they were equally as stumped.

And then it struck Mackenzie.

"What's happening on the navs?"

Alicia broke out of the daze which the message had apparently brought on. She quickly shifted her attention to the navigational screens. Even though Mackenzie had no idea yet how to operate the navigational screens with any fluency, she could tell that Alicia shared her lack of skill.

The way that Alicia fumbled several times, unable to bring up the map which would show the direct surroundings of the ship. Finally, though, she managed to get there.

The three of them stood back and stared at the navigational screens.

And saw the object approaching them quickly.

Even though it was nothing more than an indistinct blob, Mackenzie knew what it represented.

She just *knew*.

Backing away from the screen, she said, "It's him." Her gaze drifted across Alicia and Louise who wore wide-eyed expressions.

"It's *him*," she repeated.

Mackenzie had learned enough during her time aboard *ZITO* to know what to do in the event of an approaching ship; if there was something else which they wanted to bring into the cargo bay for further inspection. She headed down to the cargo bay and went through the protocols, surprised at how fluent she was—how at one with the ship she *already* was.

She checked over the proximity screens as she went, making sure that the approaching object—the approaching *ship*—hadn't been a mere mirage . . . one which had taken her, Alicia and Louise all in. The ship continued its approach.

It was made easier that everything about the airlock was automated. She had only to tap a button which would do all of the hard work concerned with reeling the approaching object into the cargo bay. She stood back and watched through the viewing window—observing as the cargo bay doors opened wide, like a pair of mechanical jaws, luring the object inside.

The ship floated on in through the gap.

It hovered for a few moments—slightly above the floor.

It certainly *was* a ship, that much was sure. She soon recognised it as an escape pod; one of the many which were present on the Celestial Stays Dome in the event of an emergency. They were kept there in case there needed to be a sudden mass-evacuation.

The pods were tough.

All of them capable of passing through Earth's atmosphere and being bashed about upon landing.

This was a good thing because, as the doors to the cargo bay shut behind the pod—and the on-board gravity reengaged—it dropped with a less than elegant *clunk*.

Mackenzie felt the vibrations pass through the floor.

A tingling sensation passed through her veins.

And trembled about her heart.

It was almost impossible to believe it.

Impossible!

And yet it seemed . . . well, there was no time to waste!

She moved quickly. She jabbed the button which released the lock on the cargo bay doors. She heard the sounds of decompression and then ran through the gap.

The door to the escape pod had hardly opened more than a fraction when she caught sight of his face.

Miguel's face!

For the longest time, she simply stood before him, the two of them taking one another in.

He reached out to her.

She felt his fingertips brush her cheek.

Her whole body went rigid and then relaxed—*in waves.*

She became super-aware of her breathing. How she breathed in profoundly. And then exhaled.

Miguel slowly closed his lips on hers, and she heard the slightest of sounds emerge from his mouth. But she understood his words. "I love you," he said. "And I always *will.*"

She held herself still for another moment, considering.

Finally, she took a step back.

Eyed him closely.

"Just how *did* you manage to get here?" she asked.

Miguel only smiled at her by way of reply. "I guess that when there's a will there's a way." He looked to the cargo bay observation window for a moment.

When she looked herself she saw that with frightening speed the entirety of the crew had assembled. She gave them all a sheepish wave. And the crew grinned back by way of response.

She took a deep breath.

Looked Miguel in the eye.

"Well, you're here now," she said.

He smirked. "Forever, actually."

She arched an eyebrow. "Second thoughts?"

"Guess there's no time for them now, huh?"

"No," she replied, taking a step closer. "I suppose *not*."

And then she gave him a kiss to remember.

A kiss to show him what he'd been *missing*.

38

ESCAPE PLAN

*K*arolin *waited* until there was a gap between shifts. It wasn't a difficult undertaking. She hardly slept these days. She had no need to consult with the Link to check who was on duty. To check that there would be no one around. It was simply a case of her sitting up in her quarters—in the middle of the night—and *listening* . . .

She heard the now-familiar *clunk-clunk* of footsteps shifting off down the corridor.

And knew this was her opportunity.

She shifted through the silent corridors. She wasn't afraid of running into anyone. She was still used to the crew holding a certain reverence for her—a certain *fear* for her.

Their memories of her being their boss still held firm, she supposed.

And it would be that way until the day she died.

Karolin made it to the cargo bay, and to the escape pod sitting there. The mechanism wasn't complicated. A simple button-press. And the internal door to the cargo bay popped open.

She glanced around. Saw that there was no one.

She continued about her work.

The escape pod hadn't been secured in any way.

She supposed that no one had given it so much as a second glance since Miguel had used it as his vehicle to arrive here—to ZITO—from the Moon.

But Karolin didn't linger too long in appreciating her good fortune.

There wasn't much time.

She was in no mood to explain her actions to others if she was discovered.

In the cockpit of the escape pod, she took in the controls—saw that it was about as simple as it had been to steal into the cargo bay itself. That was good. She never had had all that much of a technical brain. Funnily enough—despite having been at the helm of perhaps the most ambitious technical venture of all human history —she felt she hadn't much of an affinity with machines.

In fact, she had often felt that they escaped her completely.

The conundrum which faced her, however, had nothing much to do with technological considerations. It was merely a practical one.

A logical puzzle.

But—already—she felt that she had cracked it.

She left the escape pod and consulted the various switches on the wall of the cargo bay. She tapped the first. This brought the door which divided the ship from the cargo bay shut.

That was good—that was a *start*.

For her next trick, she flipped another button.

This only succeeded in causing the cargo bay lights to flicker and then go out. She jabbed that button again, smiling to herself and shaking her head at her foolhardy, monkey-handed methods.

When she hit the next button in the sequence, a calmly spoken countdown sounded through the speakers of the cargo bay. The external doors would open in sixty seconds.

Sixty seconds was *far* more time than she needed.

She returned to the escape pod, and to the cockpit.

She sat at the controls.

And shut the pod doors.

It was only now that she felt the gravity of what she was doing —of what she was *about* to do.

This was her time.

The time when she would truly cut herself free.

This was what she had always wanted.

This was what she had always *dreamed* of . . .

Outside the escape pod, she heard the speaker reach the end of the countdown.

There was a low-level groaning sound as the cargo bay doors opened.

She carefully worked the thrusters.

Eased the craft out through the doors.

And—just like that—she was floating in space.

She breathed gently—*evenly*.

She had never seen the point of getting carried away.

Not even when she was this close to death.

Slowly, she reached down for the throttle then let it out.

Put distance between herself and *ZITO*.

Gradually leaving the *ZITO*—and its crew—behind.

Forever.

39

MISPLACED MEMBER

ackenzie woke with a smile lining her lips.

For a few seconds, she wasn't quite certain where she was.

And then it all returned to her.

ZITO . . . she was on *ZITO*.

She looked to Miguel—saw that he was still sleeping.

It was then that she noticed there was a message awaiting her on the Link.

Absentmindedly—more a reflex than a definitive decision—she opened it.

The message was from Frau Köhler:

Goodbye.

To begin with, Mackenzie wasn't sure what to make of this single word. She tried to cobble together the pieces. And felt none the wiser.

'Goodbye'?

It was as she studied the message in her mind's eye that Miguel stirred beside her. He sleepily reached out a hand for her, taking hold of her thigh and giving it a squeeze. She was almost unaware of the gesture. It seemed almost to *roll* over her. To be happening on another plane of existence. A sudden sense of urgency struck her. She shrugged off the duvet.

And rushed out of her personal quarters—pausing only briefly to yank the overalls she had left in a pile on the floor up over her naked body.

When Mackenzie reached the bridge, every other member of the crew was there.

She could tell—by their expressions; how they were all glued to various screens—that something alarming had happened.

Although she had a sneaking feeling just what the issue was, she still asked the question. "What's wrong?" she asked. "What's the problem?"

In the end, it was Gofreddo who turned away from his screen to respond.

"It's Karolin Köhler," he said. "She's missing."

"And the escape pod too," Alicia put in.

Mackenzie remained standing there, behind them. She heard footsteps. When she turned she saw it was Miguel. He looked like he had hurried himself into getting out of bed and getting dressed into his overalls as much as she had. She was glad to feel his gentle, firm grasp on her shoulder.

To sense his kiss against the side of her neck.

It warmed her.

Gave her *much-needed* warmth.

"Fred?"

Everyone looked in Kyra's direction.

She was scrutinising security footage.

"What?" Gofreddo said, leaving his position and heading over to where Kyra sat.

Everyone on the bridge—Mackenzie included—turned their attention onto Kyra.

Kyra glanced up a touch self-consciously. Then she seemed to regain her sense of composure. Her sense of *confidence.* "I've got the tape," she said, and then pointed to the screen. "Look."

All of the members on the bridge looked to where Kyra pointed.

Mackenzie felt a tingling sensation run up her spine.

Miguel was no longer touching her.

Silently, the whole crew watched on as Karolin Köhler entered the cargo bay, got into the escape pod and then flew off out into space.

"Can you track her?" Gofreddo asked, a touch of panic to his voice.

"I'm looking," Kyra replied, switching to the navigational screens. She scanned the map surrounding the ship then ran it back several hours to when Frau Köhler had departed through the cargo bay. "I . . ." Kyra began. "She's gone . . . off the screens . . . off our radar."

Nobody said anything.

Then Gofreddo addressed Patrick—sitting in the pilot's chair. "Set course for the last-known coordinates," he said. "We can outgun her if we can get somewhere up to full speed."

Patrick remained frozen at the controls for several moments. Almost as if he was some sort of droid which was malfunctioning.

He looked to the others, finally settling on Mackenzie, as if she might be the only voice of reason capable of standing up to Gofreddo.

It was then that Mackenzie felt Miguel take hold of her hand. He squeezed it with his own. She felt another warmth pass through her blood.

And she knew she *had* to speak up.

She looked Gofreddo in the eye, then said, "We need to let her go—she wanted to leave for a reason. We have no grounds to pursue her like some criminal."

Gofreddo parted his lips to respond but said nothing.

Everyone on the bridge surely understood—just as Mackenzie did—that Frau Köhler had wanted things this way. She had wanted to end things *alone* . . .

As if to put an end to a prearranged meeting, Gofreddo met Mackenzie's eye, gave the trace of a smile, and then a nod. He made his way off the bridge but before he left them behind completely he paused and said—in a tone of voice which only Mackenzie could hear—"That's the reason I wanted you on this ship. You've got balls—*balls* to call me out."

With that, he stalked off the bridge and to his personal quarters.

Mackenzie stood stunned for the longest time, unsure quite what she should do with this information—that which Gofreddo had just imparted to her.

In the end she decided that the best course of action was for her just to be content with it . . .

To take the comment for what it was.

And to *savour* it.

Later on, Mackenzie ventured down to the cargo bay.

Because it seemed like the natural thing to do, while standing at the observation window, within the ship, she opened up the cargo bay doors and stared out into space for the longest time.

To start with, she wondered if she was trying to *physically* see the escape pod retreating into the darkness of space. She wondered if she wanted to see Frau Köhler *one last time* . . . and she also realised that the idea was just as ridiculous as it sounded within her own mind.

Soon enough, she heard footsteps approaching along the corridor.

She had no need to look up to see who it was.

But his identity was confirmed when he stood behind her.

When she felt his warm breath against the back of her neck.

And his steady, unwavering touch against her forearms.

He said nothing.

There was no need for words.

They had a whole *eternity* for words.

Now was a time to think.

And to dream.

And to *love*.

THE END

AUTHOR'S NOTE

Thank you for taking the time to read one of my books. If you would like to hear about my latest releases you can sign up for my newsletter here: www.essiepowers.com

Thanks for reading!

Essie Powers

Celestial Phase
The Fifth Lunar Lovescape Novel

www.ingramcontent.com/pod-product-compliance
Lightning Source LLC
Chambersburg PA
CBHW031216260626
47169CB00007B/2079